MW01170783

ROMANCING BLAKE

A ROMANTIC COMEDY

JEN ATKINSON

books

ALSO BY JEN ATKINSON

<u>Young Adult Romance</u>

Paper Hearts

The Untouched Trilogy

Untouched

Unknown

Undone

<u>Sweet Romance</u>

Then Came You

Am I 30 Yet?

Surviving Emma

Love, In Theory

The Amelia Chronicles

Knowing Amelia

Love & Mercy

Dear Kate

Because of Janie

ROMANCING BLAKE

CHAPTER ONE

Juliana

*B*lake hadn't returned my texts or calls in two days—TWO! I understand not texting back her boss or even Dad, but me? I'm her one and only sister—one and only *sibling* in fact. How could she just ignore me?

I stormed down 16th Street, my four-inch heels clicking on the sidewalk on this sunny Denver day. I knew this street well. I could pass by the tourists, the building murals, the guy with purple hair who always juggled on the corner of 16th and Lincoln without any distraction. I was focused.

I shoved open the door to *Much Ado About Cakes* bakery and stepped onto the teal and white tiled floor. The smell of sugar, flour, and sweetness filled my insides, making my mouth water.

I swallowed down the craving—I could get a Black Bottom cupcake another day—I had a bone to pick, and I wouldn't let chocolate cake with cream cheese filling and vanilla bean frosting distract me from my mission.

Blake stood there, her chestnut hair up in its usual messy bun, her elbow resting on the edge of a Kitchen Aid mixer as it churned up a deep blue batter. She watched the blue goo, mesmerized. She almost looked joyful watching that batter.

I hadn't seen that look on my sister's face in months... then again, *mischievous* joy and pure joy are different. Her eyes held mischief.

"Hello, Juliana," she said in a sing-song voice—her eyes never leaving the batter.

I faltered with her words, but only for a second. I wouldn't let her magical hearing or the eyes in the back of her head sway me from my goal.

"Hello, Blake. I'm surprised you even know how to say hello. I thought you'd forgotten." I set one hand to my hip. I purposely wore my "power" outfit. The one I wore whenever I pitched a project to a new client. I designed the slim, black and white striped pants with the matching criss-cross top myself. A one-of-a-kind— only because no matter how much Mark begged—I wouldn't sell him the design. This one was mine.

Blake's brow furrowed with my greeting and she finally looked up from the mixing bowl. She slowed the mixer to speed one, leaned back against the counter, and crossed her arms over the red apron covering her *Much Ado About Cakes* tee. "The power outfit? Really? Either I'm getting good news or your about to show me who's boss."

I leaned my hip against the edge of the metal counter, facing her, and drummed my long nails on the bakery countertop. "I have called you three times."

"You know I don't check my voicemail."

"I have texted six times."

She gave me a non-caring, one-shoulder shrug. "My cell must be dead."

"For the past two days?"

"I've been avoiding all things electronic. You know how I get."

2

I swallowed back the reply I *wanted* to give and pulled my cell from my designer pants pocket.

She rolled her eyes as she watched me find her face on speed dial and lift my finger. Dramatically—for effect—I flicked her picture and waited. *Bitter Sweet Symphony* began to blare from Blake's apron pocket.

"Dead, huh?"

She huffed out a breath and tossed her head back. "I've been busy okay?" She turned her attention back to the mixer, smacking the lever to turn the thing off. "Everyone and their dog in this city thinks they need a *gender reveal* cake." She gagged on the last three words.

"So, what's wrong with that?" I glanced at the bright blue batter in her bowl.

"It's stupid. Just let the doctor tell you or don't. But don't make your baker do it."

Was this really about a gender reveal or did Blake just hate having to be involved with everyone else's happy news?

I glanced down at the white envelope next to where my drumming fingers had been. My brows cinched together with the large G poking out from the wrapper. "Is this it? The card the couple gave you?"

Blake shrugged again, fluttering her long dark lashes—not seeming to care. But I knew better.

"Blake, this says," I pulled the card out, just to be sure, "this says *girl* on it."

She leaned over and peeked at the white index card in my hands. "Sure does."

"But," I gave my head a quick shake, "your cake is blue."

A wicked smile broke across her face. "It sure is."

"*Why* is your cake blue?" I slammed the card onto the counter, my hand flat and flush to the paper.

"If you ask a third party to tell you something—something you

3

should have asked your doctor to tell you—you can't get upset when they get it wrong!"

"Yes, you can!"

"Nobody has so far. In fact, I'm pretty sure they're blaming their doctor or whoever wrote the note."

"Blake!"

"What?" She yanked the mixing bowl from the stand and poured the sapphire blue batter into two round pans. "I don't mess them all up. I take a guess and sometimes I get it right and other times—" She smiled at the raw cake in her pans. "Sometimes, I don't."

I set the tips of my fingers to my temple. My sister! "These people are planning, Blake. They buy things, they prepare—all based on this reveal."

"*Then*," she said, tipping her head and drawing out the word, "they shouldn't have asked their baker to deliver the message."

I sighed. This is not how I wanted this conversation to go. I'd hoped to talk her into going to the Kucho's dinner party with me. But I had not guilted her into anything. I'd only argued with her—argued and lost!

"Blake," I said, mentally starting over. "The Kucho's are having a dinner party and—"

"No way. I am *not* going to that."

"Blake, I can't go alone—you know I can't. Melanie Kucho is always trying to set me up with her son and I—I'm not interested. If you're there, then I won't have to talk to her—or to him —alone."

She bent and slid the cakes into the oven. "I don't do dinner. I don't do people. You know that, Jewels."

I pressed my lips together, unsure if I should cross this line. "You... used to."

She darted a glare my way.

"And," I said before she could argue and win again, "you owe me. I covered for you last time Dad wanted a one-on-one."

4

"Juliana!" she bellowed, standing upright, hands flying to her hips.

I crossed my arms and tapped the toe of my Jimmy Choo heels. "Shall I quote?" I lowered my voice—though Blake didn't speak unnaturally low. "Get me out of this, Jewels, and I will owe you one. Big time!" Blake loved our father—as much as I did. What's not to love? However, she could not take another pep talk from Dad. And, I'd saved her butt that night.

"You are the most annoying little sister—"

"But you love me." I smiled wider than I ever should.

"Fine." Her brows furrowed. "Then we're even!"

The quiet shop's bell rang. *Much Ado About Cakes* was a made-to-order shop, so the only customers who came in were there to pick up a special request or to order for a later date. The couple stood on the teal and white tiled floor, on the opposite side of the counter as us. The woman's protruding stomach made me grit my teeth and pinch my lips.

She glanced at me, but she clearly needed Blake. "Hi!" she said, too much cheer in her voice. I could mentally hear Blake vomiting. "We wanted to order something special—a *gender reveal* cake! You know… one of those cakes expecting parents cut into. It's either blue or pink on the inside to reveal the gender of the baby." She said the words as if this were a novel idea, as if she'd just thought the idea up—here and now.

"Wow," Blake said, her tone flat. Her eyes slid to me, her blinks long and cantankerous.

"We'd like it next week if possible."

Blake breathed in through her nose, filling her chest. "Sure. How's Thursday?" She stepped over to the laptop at the end of the counter.

"Thursday!" squeaked the woman, glancing at the man beside her. "Perfect!"

"Perfect," Blake repeated in a tone that nowhere matched the expecting mother's. "I can have it ready by four."

5

The woman caressed her belly. "Great. Here's our secret!" She held out a sealed envelope. "You'll be the first to know." She giggled as if she'd given Blake a gift.

"Oh yay!" Blake scrunched her nose and offered a false smile. "Well, my guess is… girl!"

CHAPTER TWO

Blake

I swiped through the three dinner-party type outfits in my armoire. Why had I let Juliana talk me into this? I hated people. I hated dinner. I hated going out.

Juliana's pretty azure eyes, watering with unshed tears appeared in my head. *You used to*, she had said. *You used to like all those things.*

I blinked and for three seconds I saw my old life. Friends, parties, work booming… *fiancé*. Without allowing another thought to creep in, I swung my palm up and smacked myself in the forehead. "Get yourself together, Blake." Thinking about the old days was a big no-no. Not to mention a waste of time.

Instead, I thought of Juliana and that Kucho boy tripping over himself to impress her.

Jewels—with her long legs, fair skin, and white blonde hair—made a lot of guys swoon. They'd drool and gawk and make utter fools of themselves while sweet Juliana stayed oblivious to it all.

Juliana worked her way into becoming the most successful

clothing designer in the western hemisphere since Mark Zudora—her boss. The guy must be brilliant, he hired my sister. And the girl had goals. She had plans. No one else's drive could compete with Juliana's. She wouldn't be distracted because some guy spent five nights a week in the gym and wanted to take her out for drinks.

I sighed. I loved that about my sister. She had strengths where I did not. I wanted to own my own bakery, yet I made stupid gender reveal cakes in Christian's bakery.

I had gotten distracted by nice eyes, false charm, and someone to hold...

As if it had a mind of its own, my hand whipped up and slapped my forehead again—snapping myself back into the present.

I snorted and flipped backward amongst my three dressy outfits. They all sucked. "Keep it together, Blake!" Where had that distraction gotten me anyway? Heartbroken and miserable.

I snatched the burnt orange dress from my closet and threw it onto my unmade queen bed. Did it really matter what I wore? I was a body for Juliana to turn to, so pushy Mrs. Kucho would leave her alone when it came to her son.

If that were the case—then maybe I should wear the hunter green dress. Sure it didn't fit, at one size too large it reminded me of wearing a large nightgown. Comfort mattered—right? I chewed on my pointer fingernail, annoyed with myself for even taking a minute to decide on something so futile.

A tap sounded on my apartment door. I ignored it and reached into my closet. Before I could snatch the green dress though, a click from the lock told me Juliana used my spare key to let herself in. Her heels clicked as she passed through my minuscule apartment living room, down the hall, and stormed straight into my bedroom.

"Ew," she said as greeting, a linen bag draped over her left arm. "You are not wearing that." She pointed to the orange blob splayed across my queen-sized bed.

"I know," I whined. "I was grabbing my green—"

"No." She swallowed and closed her eyes in an overly dramatic fashion. "Not that one either. I brought you something," she said, with a toothy smile. "You get to wear this tonight." She held up the garment bag and unzipped it.

I stared at the little thing in her hands. "Why are there so many plants on it?"

A raspberry blew from her lips. "This is a Mark Zudora original. Do you know what the average person would pay to wear this?"

"Nothing—the average person wouldn't wear it."

She fluttered her lashes, rolling her eyes up to my ten-foot ceiling. "Shut up and take your sweats off." She set one hand to her hip, popping her bare knee with the motion. She looked as if she were ready for a photo shoot—and she didn't even realize it. To her, getting dressed was like painting a picture or writing a novel—it was art.

"Where are the pants?"

"Pants?" She looked at me as if I'd gone crazy. "This is a dress, Blake."

"A dress? But it's so short!" I pointed at her colorful, flowing skirt. "Why do you get to cover your thighs?"

She threw back her head. "Ugh. You have fantastic legs, Blake, but they aren't the longest. Wear this dress," she held up the garment bag, "and these shoes," like a magician, she whipped out a pair of four-inch heels from behind her back, "and you'll look amazing. Your legs will look long and lean."

My turn to, "*Ew.* What am I? A piece of meat?"

She leaned in, her blonde hair falling in waves over her shoulder. "You are a masterpiece." Juliana thrust the garment bag into my hands. "Get dressed, I'm doing your hair in five minutes." She strode from the room, the violet high heels she'd brought me, hanging from her fingers.

"I already fixed my hair!" But my words were lost, bouncing off her back.

I held up Juliana's dress—or I guess I should say Mark Zudora's dress. The modest, round neckline and cap sleeves I could live with. But the garden print lazily growing all over the thing made me squirm. *Weird.* Most of all though, I stressed over the length. Why did everyone at the Kucho's need to see my knees and half my thighs? *Oh right,* for fashion's sake. Lame.

I slipped into the dress and somehow it fit perfectly—even comfortably. I mean, perfect for someone who wanted to show too much leg. Still, how did Juliana do that?

Barefoot, I trudged out of the room. I flapped my arms at my sides, throwing a twenty-eight-year-old tantrum. My silent glare shouted, *Happy now?*

Juliana's head poked from the bathroom door, "In here," she said.

"Ugh." I groaned, but I didn't want to argue and lose, so I kept my mouth shut, slinked into the bathroom, and plopped myself onto the edge of the bathtub.

"Turn," she said, all business. I shifted on the tub, so she had a better angle to reach my hair, and the torture began.

Thirty minutes later she stepped back, her full lips puckered, and she waved one hand, motioning me to stand up. "Shoes," she barked—my own personal fashionista drill sergeant.

I sighed, but stood and slipped into the ridiculous heels. I faltered to the left, arms flailing, but caught myself, finding my balance. I glared at her—I'd break an ankle in these shoes!

But Juliana's lips curved into a satisfied smile as her eyes roved from my head to my toes.

CHAPTER THREE

Jack

*J*uliana had accepted my mother's invitation—and she'd checked her *plus one* box.

Plus one? Who could be Juliana's plus one? For as long as I'd known her—thirteen months and twelve days, she'd never mentioned a boyfriend. I'm pretty sure she hadn't even been on a date. At least not one that didn't include work somehow. Her Instagram and Tik Tok feeds seemed to send a single vibe. Or maybe they sent a *fashion* only vibe. Then again, maybe she sent *zero* vibes and I'd gone insane.

When I'd scrounged up my courage and asked her out, she wanted to know what type of apparel I'd be needing. When I'd told her I didn't need fitted for anything, she just looked at me confused, then changed the subject.

I snagged a look down at my Rolex. I'd never known Juliana to not be on time. I clenched my fists and nonchalantly glanced at the front entrance to my mother's terrace, the space she'd prepared— or had Matthieu prepare—for people to enter the party.

"Okay, Jackie, who are you waiting for?"

"Don't call me that," I shoved Royce's propped elbow from my shoulder.

He dropped his arm dramatically with my removal, then stood straight, brushing his hands together. "Geez, you're being a little sensitive, don't you think?"

"No, *Roy-boy*," I said, using his mother's nickname for him— two could play that game, "I'm not."

Roy grimaced, his dumb handsome face scrunching with my words. It was a good look on him—or *not* so good—which is probably why I liked it so much. Royce may be my cousin, but we didn't resemble one another, not even a little bit. Royce got all of the Kucho ruggedness, while I got my father's average height, school boy looks, and mediocre talents. Mom tried to convince me I was extraordinary, but she was wrong, and really, we both knew it. I mean, she wouldn't even take Dad's last name. Even *it* had been too average—*Anderson*. She couldn't risk losing her following when she'd already worked so hard to become *someone*. Dad meant everything to us, but the rest of the world didn't care one wit about Mackenzie Anderson.

"So, who is she?" Royce asked—waking me from my trance.

"I don't know what you're talking about," I said, as my eyes, like an automatic lighthouse, beamed over at the entrance once more. I had kept my feelings about Juliana to myself.

Roy laughed. "Sure you don't." He crossed his arms over his tailored, black suit, and watched the entry with me.

I cleared my throat, my body not willing to turn around and prove him wrong. No part of me wanted to risk not knowing when and whom Juliana entered with. "Ah, Mom asked me to keep a look out for the couturier."

A smile teased at Royce's mouth—he didn't produce an actual grin. I hated when he did that. Like he knew something the rest of us didn't. "*Right*. Your *mother* asked you to watch for her."

I shrugged, playing it cool. "You know how Mom is. If Char-lotte's dress isn't perfection, the day will be ruined."

Royce snorted out a short laugh. I'm not sure he bought my excuse, but he knew my mother, almost as well as I did. He knew she didn't accept anything less than perfection. Anyone who worked at *The Creative Drive* knew this, and Roy and I had been there since we were sixteen.

I glanced his way. "Why don't you just—"

Royce blew out a quiet whistle. "Speaking of perfection."

I whipped my head back to the entrance where...yep. *"Julianna,"* I whispered—unintentionally. Juliana's sage green skirt flowed about her legs, her hair bouncing white-gold waves at her shoulders.

"Wait, that's her?" Royce laughed as if I'd announced that I'd be climbing Mount Everest—in my suit, tie, and Oxfords. "Oh, buddy. Good luck there. You're gonna need it."

I could have played the—*I don't know what you're talking about* card again. But my heart wasn't in it. Royce was right. "I know," I said, staring ahead. He was right. I didn't stand a chance. But, oh did I want to.

Royce smacked me on the back and when I looked over at him, his expression had softened. "Well, don't just stand here. Be a good host. Go welcome the girl."

I swallowed and squared my shoulders. "Right," I said again, a glutton for punishment.

I shoved one hand into my suit pants pocket and strode over to where she stood on the grass, taking in the terrace and yard. The entire thing shimmered with what Matthieu called "twinkle lights". I looked about the space, seeing it with new eyes as Juliana saw it for the first time. She'd been to the house a dozen times, but this was her first time out back, with Matthieu having worked his magic. I knew Juliana's keen eye would appreciate it.

Her sapphire eyes sparkled as they swept over the space. She linked her arm through another's and my heart twisted, but then—

a *girl*. A girl, who, though darker in every way—hair, skin, even expression—resembled Juliana. I swore they had identical noses. A cousin maybe?

The knot in my gut eased a little with the idea. I propelled my feet forward, but I wasn't quick enough. Mom beat me there.

"Juliana!" she sang. "Darling girl." She held her hands out to Juliana, making the small crowd of mingling people part.

A stiffness took over Juliana's expression. The girl next to her pressed her lips together—as if stopping herself from laughing.

"Ven aquí!" Mom loved speaking her native dialect to Juliana—who'd spent time in Spain, but Juliana didn't speak fluent Spanish. She never returned anything vocally in the romance language, though she seemed to understand Mom's directions.

Juliana smiled—though slightly forced—and made her way to my waiting mother. The girl at her side dropped her arm and seemed to plant her feet. She would not be beckoned over.

Mom's voice quieted, but I could see as she pointed to where my sister, Charlotte, and her fiancé, Eric, sat. Almost cheek to cheek with Juliana, she straightened up. "Where is Jack? I know he's around here somewhere. He's been waiting for you and—ah! Jackie! Come here, Jackie. Juliana has arrived."

I gulped, feeling ten years old. Juliana's closed-lipped grin strained even more. The few times it had been just the two of us, I swear she relaxed and her real smile came out. Or maybe my hopeful head made it all up.

"Jack is the perfect person to show you around my garden. You and your... friend?"

"Oh," the awkward mask seemed to shatter and one of Juliana's true, perfect smiles produced. "My sister!"

Her sister—that's right, Juliana did have a sister.

"Melanie, I wanted to introduce you." She looked back at the pretty brunette. "Blake." Juliana gave a little nod and when the girl didn't move from her spot next to the entrance, her voice turned louder. "Blake!" She tilted her head and I think she even glared for a brief second. "Ven aquí!" She cleared her throat and gave a nervous laugh. "She's a little shy."

Blake trudged over, her foot stumbling, but she was quick to catch herself. She stood next to her sister—not as tall, not as elegant, not nearly as graceful, but I could still make out the resemblance. Pretty chestnut hair ran down her back and her skin, while not as porcelain as Juliana's, seemed kissed by the sun—she might have been beautiful, if she'd stop scowling.

"Blake, this is Melanie Kucho and her son, Jack."

Blake looped her arm through Juliana's once more—I think because the girl may have needed help walking in her atrocious heels.

"A Mark Zudora original?" Mom looked Juliana's sister up and down. "Very nice, Juliana. I can tell who dressed this girl."

"I know I didn't do it," Blake said, her tone snarky as she held a hand to her stomach.

Mom looked confused at the comment, but Juliana ignored her. "Blake is a baker. Her technique is fantastic. The best in the city."

Mom looked appraisingly at Juliana's sister. Her eyes turned to slits and her mouth turned down with her examination—a work face. "Do you own your own business?"

Blake cleared her throat, then shook her head. "I work for Christian McKay at *Much Ado About Cakes*."

"Hmm," she said in a tone that meant she no longer found interest in what Juliana's sister had to say. "I've never heard of him."

"Aren't you and Charlotte still looking for a baker," I said, reminding everyone of my presence.

Mother's slitted gaze shifted my way. While Blake stood straighter, her hazel eyes looking interested for the first time since their arrival. Juliana's stare seemed to find me more directly; a soft glimmer, I'd never seen before, shining through.

"No dear, we are not," my mother said—disturbing the gleam

from Juliana's shining eyes. "You know nothing of wedding plans —so don't interfere."

Nothing of wedding plans? That's all she and Charlotte ever talked about. Well, that and work. Maybe I didn't know how to plan a wedding, but I knew plenty of the plans they had already made and even the plans they still worked on.

"Don't bother yourself," Mom said, her tone sweet. "Tonight we enjoy ourselves. Tomorrow, we'll get to work." She winked at Juliana. "Jackie can show you around. He really is the dearest." She smiled at Juliana again before hopping off to find someone else equally important.

I faced Juliana, my heart speeding up just a bit. "Hey," I said— stupidly. "Glad you could come. And I'm so glad you brought your sister." I realized after the fact that I sounded much too relieved, but the words were out and I couldn't take them back. "I can show you—"

"Jack," Juliana chuckled lightly. "You don't have to babysit us. Really, we're fine." She beamed. "Go enjoy yourself."

"Oh. Right." I nodded. Then, shoving my hands into my pockets, I took one step backward. "Sure. Have a good night."

I took two more steps backward and watched as Juliana and her sister walked the opposite direction. One more step and I bumped straight into—

"That was quick."

"Royce. What are you— Have you been watching me?"

"I just happened to notice that you didn't say much and now they're gone. Call it an observation."

"Yeah, well she's with her sister and I didn't want to interrupt them."

"Ah, her *sister*. Nice—for you, I mean. At least your chances are at two percent instead of negative twenty-two percent."

I scoffed out a bitter laugh. "Yeah."

"I'm kidding," he said, hitting me in the shoulder. "Listen, I'm gonna help you out. Sisters tell each other *everything*. They *just* saw you, no doubt they're talking about you. I'll go stand by them and see what they have to say."

"What? No, I mean—that's terrible and—"

"Everything, Jack. *Everything.* You want to know what's in this girl's head, you need to know what she's telling her sister."

"Everything?" I said, for a brief second considering his offer.

Royce's brows rose as his lips hinted at a conspiratorial grin.

I searched the grassy ground we stood on for a second, twinkle lights making the green a dark forest color. "I—no, that's sick. Royce," I looked up. "Royce!" But he was already headed toward Juliana.

CHAPTER FOUR

Royce

$\mathcal{I}$ made a beeline for the waiter holding the flutes of bubbly liquid. Sure, *that's* why I crossed the yard. I picked up a glass and held it close to my chest. I wouldn't ingest the liquid—I was never much of a drinker. But I'd hold it and pretend to mingle while I stood near Jack's crush. I'd do it for two reasons—one, messing with Jack brought me great joy—he just made it so easy. If my cousin weren't a true blue nice guy and my best friend, I'd find myself jealous as heck and in absolute hate with the guy. But, I loved Jack—most of the time, anyway. Reason number two, what else was I supposed to do at one of Aunt Melanie's fancy parties?

If I didn't work for her, if I weren't dying to be promoted— the promotion I was 99% certain would go to Jack, I wouldn't be here at all. But I *did* work for her, I *did* want to find grace in her sight, and I couldn't let Jack suffer all night by himself—or maybe I couldn't resist the opportunity to make Jack suffer a little more. This had to be killing him, watching me listening in, waiting for what would *never* happen. Why would this girl ever talk about—

"You said only the mother wants you to date what's-his-name." The cynical brunette downed her bubbly drink and seemed to search for another waiter.

"*Jack*, his name is Jack," said my cousin's infatuation.

"Yeah, well, you were wrong. The guy has it bad." The brunette shook her head and searched her cup for another drop.

"Has what bad?" the girl asked, her tone sweet and sincerely innocent.

"Juliana, I realize I'm one year older and wiser, but come on. Tell me you aren't totally blind!"

I stepped an inch closer—this might be more entertaining than I thought.

"I'm not blind, Blake. And you don't need another drink." She took the flute glass from her sister. "He's as much a victim in this as I am. It's all his mother. Believe me. Every time we make an appointment, she summons Jack to her side. He works for her and—"

"He works for his *mommy?*" Blake snorted. "That's a little pathetic."

"Why?" Juliana set a hand on her curved hip. "He's good at what he does. He enjoys it. Who cares if his mother's his boss?"

"I'd want to make it on my own." Blake swallowed and scratched at her neck as if this conversation suddenly made her uncomfortable. "What does *Melanie* do anyway? What makes her so high and mighty?"

I snorted into my chest at the girl's description of Aunt Melanie.

"Believe me, she has reason to be high and mighty. She started her own web design company at age twenty-five. By thirty-five *The Creative Design* had hit the top ten of the world's most successful web designers. *And,*" Juliana—taller than her sister, dipped her head, "she's the only female in that top ten."

Blake's brows rose, her interest sincere now. "Wow. Okay. Consider me impressed."

I blew air into my cheeks as I listened to them. Yes, Aunt Melanie had a pretty sweet resume. No one could deny that.

Juliana continued. "When she got married, she kept her maiden name, it already meant something in the world of web design. She had two kids, Charlotte and Jack, but never stopped working. She now has six branches across the US and one in her home country of Spain."

"She's Spanish? I couldn't even tell."

"She doesn't have an accent. She grew up speaking two languages. She really is brilliant." Juliana blew out a sigh.

"And she's certain you'd be perfect for her son?" Blake made a face at her sister, her smile too toothy, her eyes too wide.

Juliana groaned. "She is."

"So," Blake shrugged, "maybe you should listen to her. You're the one who called her brilliant."

No way—this could not be happening. I peered a little closer at Juliana's sister. Was Jackie about to get a date?

"I can't believe *you*, of all people, would say that." Juliana stared at her sister, her mouth gaping open.

Blake rolled her eyes. "That's because we both know it's a load of crap. I didn't mean it, just because some millionaire—"

"*Multi-millionaire*," Juliana corrected her.

Blake cleared her throat. "*Multi-millionaire* wants to play match-maker doesn't mean you should listen. Love is something people tell you that you need to be happy. But it isn't true. Love brings more misery than it gives happiness. You know that Jewels."

Ahh—a *true* romantic. I'm guessing Blake never played princess or knight in shining armor as a child.

"And you know this by experience?" Juliana met her sister eye to eye.

"You know I do!" Blake practically shouted at her.

"Right," Juliana said, crossing her arms, "because you're just so happy, *now*."

A waiter walked by and Juliana set Blake's empty flute onto his tray. Blake reached out, stealing another filled cup before he could get away. Then she blew a sigh from her chest. "I'm *not* happy." She looked into the barrel of her goblet before downing the sparkling drink. "We both know that. And we both know *why*." She dropped her hand that held her empty cup, and flapped it against her side. Then, holding the flute up and jiggling it between her fingers, she said, "I'll be back. I'm empty again."

Juliana watched after her sister as if no one else existed. A stress, that hadn't shown before, sparked in her eye.

"What are you doing?" Jack said, suddenly at my side. He tugged on my sleeve, hissing in my ear.

"Dude, I'm getting info. Good stuff."

Jack rolled his neck, his eyes darting to Juliana just feet away from us. Though her gaze stayed locked on her sister, yards away —now seated at the bar. "Did—did she say anything about me?"

I tilted my head, happy to give him a mischievous grin. "She did."

His fingers fished at my jacket. "She did?" he whispered. "What? What did she say?"

"She doesn't have a clue that you have any feelings at all, little cousin. She is one hundred percent certain your mom is behind it all."

His brows furrowed and he looked past me into space. "Huh. Really? I—I thought I made it clear, and that she just wasn't interested, but then…" Jack trailed off. "Huh."

"Her sister told her to go for it. For *you*." I gave him a grin, waiting, with elation, for what would be a hilarious response.

His eyes brightened and his smile radiated.

And guilt punched me in the gut—okay, maybe I'd messed with Jack enough. I opened my mouth to tell him about the cynical girl —she didn't believe in love—she didn't mean any of it.

"What did she say?" Jack asked. But before I could answer the idiot threw caution to the wind and called, "Juliana! Hey, Juliana, over here."

The pretty blonde turned, meeting Jack's giant smile.

I nudged his side and growled out under my breath, "She never said she liked you back."

"She never said she didn't," Jack said, still showing all his perfectly straight teeth in a beam.

But his brows furrowed as Juliana wiped a single tear from her eye. Composing herself, she strode over, her sage green skirt, short in the front and long in the back flowing as she walked. Did she design the clothes or wear them on a runway?

Yep, Jack knew how to pick a pretty girl. But he needed to learn how to pick a girl who might reciprocate his feelings.

He must have been truly smitten because before I could protest again, he was gone—meeting her halfway.

I glanced over at the sister—I'd heard enough to know she wasn't happy... or innocent. She stood at the bar, pointing to a bottle the bartender had yet to open.

Curious, my legs moved me forward to where the cynical girl stood. The bartender seemed relieved to have a different patron arrive.

"Champagne sir?" He tried to keep his eyes steady on me, but they darted to Blake who attempted to lap up the last drop from her flute.

"Club soda," I said, nodding at the man.

"I'll take his champagne!" Blake said, bobbing in place. For the first time since I'd been watching her, she smiled. The thing blared —obnoxious—as if she meant to eat you with it. It held no sweetness—like her sister's smile. Of course... that could have been the alcohol smiling.

"Uh—" the bar tender's mouth drooped.

"Go ahead. She can have mine." I waved a hand toward him.

22

Aunt Melanie spent a fortune on parties like these, she had plenty of champagne.

"You are a s-saint," Blake said, slurring her s. Everything felt a little on the creepy side—I knew her name, I knew her relation, but she didn't know me from Adam.

I ran my finger and thumb over the beard on my chin. "I'm really not."

She laughed. "You're right. You aren't. I can tell." She attempted to whisper, but nothing came out quiet.

"Oh, yeah? How is that?" I leaned against the bar, crossing my arms over my chest and watching her.

"Your beard."

"My beard?"

"Yes," she threw a hand my way, "it's short, trimmed to perfection, and supposed to be like one of those lame messy buns. Women pretend to just throw their hair up when really it takes them twenty minutes to accomplish the look." She cupped her hand and whispered, "Fake-o-la!"

"My beard is like a *fake* messy bun?"

"Is that offensive to you?" She pursed her lips and narrowed her eyes on me.

"I mean… *maybe.*"

Who was this girl? She meant to insult me—within five minutes of meeting me?

Blake laughed, rolling her head backward. "You think women everywhere will fall in love over a handsome face?"

"Who said anything about love? I gave you a drink, Miss."

She blew out a long breathy sigh. "And now you deserve my devotion? You are the kind of man who thinks he can come in and sweep a woman off her feet. I can see it in your eyes."

"And in my beard," I muttered under my breath.

She snapped at the bartender, as he opened another bottle for her promised drink. "But we don't need you to sweep, Mr. Beard!"

"Or vacuum, I hope." I ground my teeth. I couldn't decide if I found her entertaining or just extremely irritating.

"Bah!" she threw her head back. "You think you're funny. You think we'll laugh and swoon and fall down at your feet because you're so stupidly handsome."

I tugged on my collar. "Well, I'm no James Bond."

"Of course, you would compare yourself to a man like James Bond."

"What's wrong with James Bond?" I turned to face her, just as she snatched her drink from the bartender. A spray of champagne fanned out from her glass, spurting over my suit coat. I hissed and snatched up a cocktail napkin, dabbing where she'd hit me.

Talk about an unpleasant human.

"James Bond is the type of man that men like you aspire to be. Someone who thinks they can fix the world with their... *manliness*. Someone who thinks that they are a gift to women everywhere. Someone who thinks that women are defenseless creatures who need saving! He is possibly the most misogynistic character in all of Hollywood." She downed her glass, but her laser beam eyes found me again. "Knowing that you like him makes me know I want nothing to do with you!"

I held up both hands. "All I did was offer you my drink."

She sputtered out a raspberry. "Well, I don't want it!"

I knit my brows and pointed at the goblet in her hand. "Um, you already drank it."

Her honey brown eyes turned to slits. "Offer me another."

"Excuse me?"

She waved her hands toward herself, rolling her head back. "Come on, Mr. Beard! Offer me another!"

I scoffed but played along with the crazy girl. "Would you like my next drink?"

She threw her head forward and pointed at me. "NO! Ha! Take that, James Bond!"

CHAPTER FIVE

Juliana

*M*y heart hurt. I had a tendency to become fixated on my goals. And I'd let my job become my everything, my one-track. Meanwhile, the sister I knew and loved died on the inside, leaving nothing but a contemptuous, angry shell. I thought taking her out for a night of fun and fancy would cheer her up, but she made it clear we were long past cheering up.

I masked my feelings when Jack Anderson requested that I join him. This wasn't the time or the place for a breakdown—especially when I had no idea how to help my sister. And I couldn't just put work away. I didn't know how to have two tracks running at the same time. My work never stopped—and I loved my work. It was an easy fixation.

"Hey," Jack said, meeting me halfway, "is everything all right?"

"Of course." I waved away his concern, grinning over my despair. "Why wouldn't it be?"

"You just—you seem sad."

"Do I?" I kept my voice steady, I kept my smile going—for me, for work. But another tear of truth fell onto my cheek. I didn't know how to take care of my sister and work at the same time. And a small monster inside of me didn't want to choose.

Jack brushed away the drop, his fingers light and soft. For the first time since I'd met him... I don't know, months ago—I looked straight into the eyes of Jack Anderson. While I didn't love that his mother, a very important client of mine, constantly tried to push us together, his hazel eyes held sincere kindness.

That kindness only made a third tear fall. I had officially lost it!

"Juliana," he said, concern in his voice, "what is it?"

I darted a glance to the side. Blake spoke to the bartender, a new drink in her hand. "I should go."

"Go? But you just got here." Jack reached out, snatching me by the fingers.

"Jack, you don't have to do this," I said. Sure, Melanie made her voice heard, above all others, but he didn't have to listen. No doubt she'd told her son to make me feel comfortable, to be extra kind to me, but he didn't need to. I didn't know why the woman had decided her son and I would go well together—but no doubt she'd pressured him into coming over here.

"Do what?" his brows furrowed. "I don't know what you mean."

"You don't have to run to my rescue just because Melanie thinks you should."

"Mel—" He shook his head. "Juliana, I'm here talking to you because I want to be. Because... because I *like* you." He blew out a breath, blinked, and found my eyes once more. "I have liked you—for a while now."

I peered at him, my gaze narrowing. I wasn't sure if I believed him. But did it matter? I could feel my composure faltering. I glanced back at Blake, unable to find a track for Jack or even work, as my sister stood at the bar drowning her misery in champagne. My one track mind had zeroed in on Blake, and Blake alone.

Jack's hand, still grasping mine, squeezed. "I—I just want you to be happy. I—"

"And I just want my sister to be happy," I cried, huffing out an honest answer. "I don't know if I can be while she's so miserable." And I don't know how to juggle it all. How can I possibly help her and work?

"What's wrong with her?" he asked, and he seemed to mean it. His words dripped with sincerity. Why had I never noticed that about Jack Anderson before?

"She—" I gulped. Blake's story wasn't mine to tell. "It's been a rough year. She could use a win." I pulled my fingers from Jack's grasp. "I'm sorry Jack. Please apologize to your mother for me." I turned away from him, doing my best to hold the tears at bay. I walked toward Blake, pretending I didn't hear Jack calling my name.

"Let's go," I said, now across the lawn. I snatched onto Blake's elbow.

"But I'm making friends." She blinked, but her eyes took too long to open the second time around.

"The bartender is not your friend, Blake."

"But he could be," she said, her voice trying to whisper but unable to. "Isn't that right, Fernando?"

"How many glasses have you had?" I chided in her ear.

She held up her hand, looking at her fingers as if trying to count, but too mesmerized by the appendages to do so.

"Come on, you can figure it out in the car."

"We have a car?" Blake said—her words slurred.

"Seriously, Blake, we've been here thirty minutes, you're already drunk?"

"Alcohol does not like me." She peered over at me, meeting me eye-level in the four-inch heels I made her wear.

"It never has. That's why you aren't a drinker—remember?"

Her brows scrunched as if trying to remember her own philosophy—and failing.

I messaged an Uber, all why ushering my sister out of the biggest account of my life, praying the entire time that Melanie

Kucho would not find me MIA. She had said this was a social gathering and we wouldn't need to discuss work. Hopefully, she'd meant it. As much as I loved my sister, as much as my heart broke with her new cynical self, I also didn't want to get fired.

Melanie Kucho had named me her daughter, Charlotte's, wedding dress designer. The public had been informed—it was like awarding me an Oscar. I prayed I hadn't just thrown it all away.

For some insane reason, I had decided to invite my sister to Charlotte's engagement party. It hadn't helped Blake—or my career.

~

"*O*kay, time for bed," I said, unzipping the back of the Zudora dress Blake wore. As if she were a child, I slid the dress from her slender body and helped her into a T-shirt.

"I like my bed," she hummed, smiling for the first time tonight.

"I know you do."

"We're best friends. My bed and me." Tears welled in Blake's eyes. "He loves me. He never leaves me."

"Blake," I sat her down—onto the bed she loved so much—and took off the lavender Tom Ford heels from her bare feet. "Don't cry, sweetie."

She splayed her fingers across the sheets of her unmade bed—the satin ones I'd given her for Christmas. "He never leaves, Jewels." She flopped down onto the queen mattress, her head hitting the pillow. "But I leave him—every single morning." A small sob fell from her chest.

Ugh. Why did she have to drink?

I rubbed her forehead with my hand. "Shh. It's okay."

"I love you, Juliana," she said, closing her eyes.

"I know, Blake." I sighed, massaging my temples. "I love you, too."

More tears leaked from my sister's closed eyes. "I miss him," she cried.

"Sweetie, you're in your bed—"

Her hands flapped, as if trying to smack the bed, but failing, and her eyes drifted open. "Not my bed, Jewels!"

"Okay," I said, putting the pieces of her puzzle together.

"I miss him, every day."

Neal. She never talked about him—unless it was to say *good riddance*—and she *never* admitted to missing him. He'd broken their engagement more than a year ago. He'd left her for someone else. He'd had an affair and she'd never suspected. That had upset her as much as his leaving.

So, she put on an angry, bored, and cynical face to hide what she didn't want anyone to see—raw and very real heartbreak.

More hot tears leaked from her eyes. I dabbed at her cheeks and kissed her head. I wanted to say—*Why? Why miss him, Blake? He doesn't deserve you.* But I didn't. I couldn't. Not when, for the first time in fifteen months, Blake exhibited an emotion other than sardonic resentment. Even if she needed champagne to finally admit her feelings.

~

I walked past a tall rugged man, working at a standing computer to the open-roomed desk where Melanie Kucho had planted herself. She usually worked in her glass office within the mix of her web designers. Open, but private. But today she sat amongst them.

"Juliana! Dearest," she crooned. "I'm in the midst of my babies today." She smiled and the man I passed snorted, pushing the glasses up on his nose. "Shush Royce, I know your mother." Melanie barked, without batting an eye.

I looked back at the man, but he kept his nose glued to his computer.

Melanie winked at me. "One moment." Lifting her cell, she sent a quick text, then set her hands to her hips, her smartphone still in her grasp. "So, the other night—"

"I know—I didn't stay long." Fessing up to what she surely already knew seemed the way to go. "My sister needed to leave. I should have known better than to bring her."

From nowhere, Jack came jogging up beside his mother. His dark blond hair waving with his run. His hazel eyes pierced me and made me remember what he'd said—*he liked me.* It wasn't his mother's doing. But Melanie proved every time we met that she'd already invested in a relationship that didn't exist. In fact, I'd bet money that she texted him to come running just now.

Besides, who had time to date? I had too many tracks running as it was… Dating? Nope, I didn't have a lane for that.

Still, he smiled as if he genuinely wanted to know when I arrived. Again, I wasn't sure why.

"It's fine. Your sister is invited every time we celebrate—though I do hope you'll linger a little longer next time."

I shook my head and gave a small shrug. "She's going through something. I should have known better—"

"Oh goodness, why do you say that?"

"Mom," Jack said, dipping his head and glowering at Melanie. "That's private."

Melanie held one hand out to me. "She's the one who said it. Besides, Juliana and I are like old friends. Aren't we dear?"

"Um, yes. We are friends." What else should I have said? "Blake's in a bit of a slump is all. She's not really herself right now."

"Melanie," a man with dark skin, white hair, and broad shoulders poked his torso from Melanie's epic glass office. "Andrew is on line one."

"Ooo—I have to take this. Jack, go over the cloth samples with Juliana."

"Cloth—mother, I don't know what you and Charlotte want."

30

"It's for the groomsman, you can figure this out. Use your right brain." She laughed and tossed back her pixie, red-dyed head.

Jack and I sat at the desk where Melanie had been. Jack's gaze darted to the man at the standing desk. He rubbed his chin, over his short dark beard, but paid us no attention.

"I'm sorry that your sister is struggling. Can I help? Charlotte went through something a couple years ago and I took her to a concert and bought her a stupidly expensive jacket."

I snickered. "No concert is going to revive Blake from this slump she's in." I rubbed my middle finger over the center of my forehead, a headache forming.

"Can I ask what she does need?"

I swallowed. "Honestly," I looked up to meet Jack's hazel eyes. They were nice eyes—I mean, if I had any time to care that they were nice. Which I didn't. "I'm not sure. She had a bad breakup. And her career isn't where she wants it to be. I think if she could do something great at the bakery, it might help her. You know? Maybe get her back on track and moving in the right direction."

Jack bit down on his thumbnail. "Huh. I mean, I know a lot of people—and they're always having some kind of celebration, or meeting, or something. I could get her some business. I'm sure of it."

I stared down at my lap. "You're sweet, Jack, but you don't have to do that. You don't even know what she does."

"She... bakes... right?"

I lifted one shoulder and bit my lip. "Right."

"Is she any good?"

I knit my brows. "Yeah. Actually, she has excellent skills and impeccable taste."

"Okay, then. I trust you." He wet his lips and peered at me intently. "Your opinion is impeccable." He rubbed his hands over his lap and looked down with the nervous twitch. "Juliana, if I did you this little favor and recommended your sister's skills to a few people, could you do me a favor in return?"

My heart fluttered. Jack would do that for me? He'd help Blake —and me. I didn't know how to help her—and work had me one thousand percent preoccupied. "Yes," I said—too quickly. My father would have disapproved.

"If I can get your sister one heck of a gig—would you consider going on a date with me?"

I swallowed—I hadn't been expecting that.

"And," he cleared his throat, "I'll do it anyway—even if your answer is no." He lifted his hand and wrapped it about the back of his neck. "Just so you know." Blowing out a breath, he said, "So, really, I guess I'm saying—I'll help your sister. *And* maybe sometime we could go out?" He shrugged, his eyes lifting to find mine again.

I had no interest in dating—there wasn't a track for that. Plus, I had no romantic ideals when it came to Jack Anderson. Still, Jack was kind. And sincere. Two things I appreciated in a person. "You really want to? That's not Melanie speaking?"

His shoulders shook and he gave a small groaning laugh. "I *really* want to."

"Okay, then. Make a recommendation," I said—stalling, going back to the offer he'd made, "get my sister an interesting bake, and we'll have dinner." I could squeeze in dinner—I had to eat, right?

His lips peeked to a grin.

"As friends," I added.

"Sure," he said, dipping his head, "as friends."

I breathed out. Jack would help me with Blake. Maybe my one-track brain wouldn't have to stress about her so much and maybe I wouldn't totally fail her. "Now, samples?" I held out the different shades of navy, black, and brown cloths for Jack to see.

He pointed to the standard mute black.

I bit my inner cheek. "How about I do you a favor and use my impeccable opinion and choose for you."

CHAPTER SIX

Jack

I sat at my desk—not working on the Beppler project, like I should be. Instead, I scrolled through a spread-sheet of our current clients and made a list of all the accounts that might be needing a celebration baked good. I needed a big account, a fantastic company that could hire Juliana's sister for a job. And I needed a web designer willing to help me out. I didn't know all these clients. I'd have to work with their designer more than anyone.

"Do you make it a habit to swindle women into dating you?" Royce took three long strides over to my desk, one hand in his pocket.

"You were listening. Of course you were." I shook my head but kept my eyes on the project at hand. "I'm not swindling her. I'm helping her. She doesn't have to date me." I swallowed—because while I wouldn't enforce the playful bargain, I still wanted the date. I wanted to help Juliana. I wanted her to look at me as more than just Melanie Kucho's son. And maybe helping her with Blake would help us get to know each other better.

"Doesn't she have big clients? Couldn't she do the same thing for her sister?"

I peered up, meeting Royce's judgmental gaze. "She—she doesn't have time. It's hard for her. She has a lot going on at work."

"Right. And you don't." He walked over to my desk and sat in the chair opposite me. "What are you working on?"

"Nothing," I said, sliding a notebook overtop the paper I wrote on.

"Big clients for Blake?" Royce snorted. "Next time you hand-write a ridiculous plan for a girl who doesn't even like you, maybe cover up the title."

"Juliana and I are friends. I'm helping a friend."

Royce let out an impatient sigh. "So, what's the plan, then?"

I adjusted in my seat, unsure if I wanted to share it with my cousin. "I'm just going to ask a designer to suggest to one of our bigger clients that they use Blake's services."

"How manipulating."

"It isn't manipulating."

"It is." He pointed at me. "It's not a bad idea. I'm surprised you came up with it, Saint Jack."

"Don't call me that. It's worse than *Jackie*."

"The question is," Royce stood and took a half seat on the edge of my desk, "how will you convince the shmuck who's over the account to help you?"

"I think most people would be willing. It's a recommendation, not a kidney. Besides, Blake's good at what she does."

"So says her sister. You don't know that." Royce crossed his arms and I wanted to shove my elbow into his bicep.

"You don't need to be here for this. I got it."

"I wanna see who you're considering." Royce moved my note-book, uncovering my handwritten list of clients.

I couldn't help it; I roamed over the list as he did. "Saint

Joseph's would be a big account," I pointed at the name I'd written, "and they have a company party coming."

Roy wrinkled his nose. "The hospital isn't exactly classy."

I ran my finger down the list. "Martinsen's? Nah, not big enough." My eyes roved over company after company. I stopped my running finger. "This is it." I tapped the paper. "The *Cherry Blossom Festival*. It's an all-day event. The city loves it. People from all walks of life come to enjoy and celebrate the Japanese culture." I began to speak faster. My gut told me—this was it! "It's advertised for months. We've been working on this web page for over a year. I'm sure of it. Who is the designer for this one again?"

Royce grunted. "You're joking, right? You're messing with me?"

I looked up, forgetting that he stood there, listening to me. "*Royce...*" I laughed. I couldn't have planned it better. He already knew the situation. I wouldn't have to have an awkward, half-truth conversation with another designer. And I wouldn't worry they'd mention anything to my mother. I stood, staring at my cousin. "Perfect."

"Not perfect. Why would I risk my biggest account in a decade so that a girl who doesn't like you can get her sardonic sister a job?"

"Because, when I turn down the VP promotion coming up in September, I'm going to remind my mother how dedicated you are to this company, how long you've been here, and how trustworthy you are. Not to mention, she loves keeping things in the family."

"Turn it down?" For the first time since he walked over to my desk, Royce sounded genuine—his eyes widened with sincerity and his tone grew eager. "Jack—you're a shoo-in. We all know that. It's like passing on the crown. You'd give that up for a *girl*?"

"I don't want the job. I never did." And I *really* liked the girl.

His eyes glossed over, I could see the wheels turning. He wanted this. He'd always wanted this. "Why?"

"It's not who I am. I'm not the boss. I'm the designer and I like where I'm at." I could see he didn't believe me. "I was planning to accept the job—out of obligation, not desire. The thing is, Juliana needs my help and I'd rather help her out than anything right now."

Royce hissed and ran a hand through his dark hair. *"Man.* Jack, you got it bad. Is she worth it?"

I nodded once, my heart thumping with the vulnerable confession. "She is."

Scratching his beard, he said, "Ugh. Little cousin. You want the girl. I want the job." He blew out a shaky breath and shrugged. "I'll help you. But I've talked to Juliana's sister. It's going to take more than a job to get that giant-sized chip off her shoulder."

"What do you mean?"

"The girl's been burned. If we could orchestrate a relationship…"

I narrowed my eyes. That didn't sound… nice.

"Hear me out," he said. "We orchestrate a relationship—or maybe a few dates, make her feel desirable again. Then she breaks up with our boy-toy chump and feels all empowered."

"What if she doesn't break up with him?"

"Ah—she will. We'll make sure she does, even if he has to be ultra-annoying. He'll be the problem in the relationship, not her." Royce rubbed his hands together as if it were a done deal. But uncertainty filled me.

Would this work? If it did—we could help everyone—me, Royce, and Blake. And hopefully, Juliana would feel helped and loved on an entirely new level.

"We just need to find us a chump," Royce chuckled.

"Oh, that we've already got." I pointed at Royce's chest. "You think I'm helping you get a promotion so someone else can get their hands dirty? This stays between you and me. I won't have Juliana or her sister getting hurt over this."

CHAPTER SEVEN

Blake

"Hey Siri," I said, with my hands covered in flour and my next gender reveal card tucked tightly in its envelope inside my apron pocket. I liked to look at the card *after* I'd guessed pink or blue. "How many babies were born in Colorado this year?"

My phone lit up on the counter and Siri's girly-mechanical voice spoke to me. "This year, there were 61,494 live births in Colorado."

I groaned. "No wonder." I looked at my jars of dye atop my counter. "Pink or blue. Hmmm... Eenie meenie miny moe—"

The bell above the shop rang. I liked the space of the shop, but I loathed baking out front for all customers to see. Blah.

A tall man with a rugged beard stepped inside. Unlike other bakeries, *Much Ado About Cakes* didn't have glass cases filled with pastries for people to come purchase. We were a make-to-order bakery.

I snatched the pink food coloring bottle from the counter and dipped my icing knife into the small jar. At this point, I could estimate any measurement for the shade I desired and be spot on. I retrieved half a teaspoon and added it to my French vanilla cake and the blending mixer. The white fluffy mixture instantly took on a bright pink hew.

The man started toward me but looked about the room—clearly looking for something to buy.

"We're an order-only bakery."

"Huh—that's what I read on the website, but come on, not even a sample?"

I smirked. "If you want a sample, you can schedule an appointment with a baker." I fluttered my lashes. "For a fee, of course."

"Of course," he smiled back, unoffended it seemed.

I frowned. I knew that smile... *How* did I know that smile?

"How does one choose a baker?"

I groaned a little and flicked off my mixer. "It's just me and Christian. What are you wanting?" I leaned against the counter, arms crossed, watching him with distrust.

"Then, I pick you." His brows rose and he murmured out, "Seeing how delightful you are."

My forehead wrinkled and my brows knit. I *did* know him! "James Bond?" All at once, the night of Juliana's dinner party came flooding back. Oh, the headache I had the next day—yet another reason I didn't normally consume alcohol. Why in the world would this guy come into *my* bakery and ask *me* to bake him something?

He laughed, his perfectly white teeth gleaming against his russet beard. "Actually, it's Royce."

"*You.* I met you the other night. You were—"

"Charming? Gracious?" He gave a one shoulder not-so-humble shrug. "I did give you my drink."

"Cocky."

"I believe you jumped right to misogynistic without even really getting to know me. It hurt." He held a mocking hand to his chest. "But I'm over it and ready to hire you."

My lip curled. I couldn't seem to look at him without judging him—but truthfully I didn't know him. But then, I didn't think I needed to know him, to know his type.

Still, I wanted to vomit at the thought of another gender reveal cake. I scanned down to Royce's left hand. No wedding band. Then again, for all I knew, he could need five gender reveal cakes for five different lady friends.

"What do you want?" I asked, unwilling to force the skepticism from my voice.

His thick brows rose again. "Well—"

Christian came in from the back kitchen. "Blake, I've got two more gender reveals for you. Call-ins. They'll be by this afternoon with their envelopes." My lanky boss lifted his head from the notes he'd written on. "Uh, hello there," he said to Royce. Christian pulled the hairnet from his graying head and smiled at Royce. "Has Blake taken your order?"

"Not yet. She was just getting to it."

"What's the event?" Christian wiped his hands on a hanging towel and crossed over to the other side of the counter, meeting Royce eye to eye—whoa, he could stand next to Christian and not peer up. My boss had to be 6'4.

"I'm looking for an attraction for the dessert table at the annual *Cherry Blossom Festival.*"

Christian's grin broadened and he peered over at me. I couldn't blame him, we were a popular bakery, but we'd never had a job from *that* big of a client. He'd never let me have that job. "Now, that's a big order. I'm Christian, the owner of *Much Ado About Cakes*. I'd love to set up a time to go over the details—"

"Actually, the *Cherry Festival* would like to work with your associate, Blake Minola, if possible."

"Blake?" Christian said, peering over at me. "Is there a reason why?"

How did he know my last name? How had he found me?

"We've heard good things."

39

Of course, Christian would ask *why Blake*—being the shop owner and a *man. Grr.* Certainly, *he* could do it better than me! My head went hot. And I wanted to shout at him that I could do anything he could—if given the chance.

I ground my teeth. *Jerk!*

Except… Christian had always been a pretty nice person. He'd never discredited me before. My biggest complaint until this very second was the gender reveal duty he had me on.

Just when my head considered cooling with kind thoughts… *Is that all he thinks I can do? Stupid gender reveals?* What a—

"She is my top baker," Christian said. My head whipped his direction.

Sure, I may have been his *only* baker, but at least he showed me merit. I knew Christian would be drooling over this new assignment, yet he didn't discredit me. I truly had always liked Christian —again, minus the gender reveal jobs—but my respect for him at that moment magnified. My feminist attacks on him died with a single sentence.

"I'm certain she can handle it," he said.

I knew Christian would be asking me a million questions and I'd be given loads of unwanted suggestions, but at least he wasn't arguing. At least he trusted me.

It looked as if I had the job! And it was a big one.

CHAPTER EIGHT

Royce

"So," I said, watching as Blake's boss retrieved to the back once more. I wasn't sure he'd ever leave us alone. "About that taste test?" I wouldn't be getting promoted if I talked the *Cherry Blossom Festival* into buying a crappy cake.

"Oh, um sure." She cleared her throat and for once had nothing snarky to say. Maybe I'd hear a little less of that now I'd officially become her client. She opened up a laptop computer at the end of the counter. "Let me look at dates. When is the event? We'd normally start something this big six months in advance."

"Well, you've got two. It's June 25th."

"Two?" she said, her snarky tone back. She glared at me as if I hadn't just given her the biggest gig of her life and as if I'd set the event date just to annoy her.

"How long does it take to bake a cake?"

She blew out a shaky breath. "That's fine. I can do this in two months."

I lifted one brow and leaned against the counter, watching her. "Is that really a problem?"

"She slammed the top of the computer down. I realize you've probably only ever watched your mother bake box mixes at home or maybe Cake Wars on TV, but a cake this big takes time. There's the tasting," she listed on her fingers, "trials so that we know I'm actually giving you what you want, securing any accents you might want, researching those details, and then of course the actual cake!"

I held my hands up in surrender. "Okay, sorry. Just a question."

"I'm just saying, two months isn't as much time as you'd think. I'll have other bakes, not just yours."

I nodded, one dramatic nod. "Noted."

She sighed and lifted the top of the computer once more. Sitting on a stool, she darted one glance my way. "Who are you, anyway? Do you work for the festival?"

"I do." I swallowed, stretching the truth—but really, only a little. "I'm a designer."

She perked up, but her tone stayed cynical. "A designer? Is that how you know Juliana?"

"Juli—?" I shrugged, pretending... poorly.

"You don't know Juliana? The party the other night—"

"Oh! The party. I know Melanie Kucho." I let an air of importance radiate from my tone. Aunt Mel *was* important. And we were pretty tight. Why not use it to my advantage?

Blake snorted. "Is that supposed to impress me?"

"You asked why I attended the party—I answered. Be impressed or don't. I don't care." I ground my teeth—was she always this frustrating?

She skittered out a fake laugh, her eyes on the computer. "Are you for real?"

"I am." I smacked my palm on the counter. "As is this job." Err— at least it would be when I convinced the Festival committee. "This is a huge event. Every year we have cherry pie, cherry cobbler, and cherry macaroons. This year, we want something extraordinary. Do you even want the job?"

Her eyes turned to slits and she didn't give me the resounding, resolute, apologetic *YES!* I'd been expecting. "Why did you pick me? You don't know me."

"I've heard good things," I repeated—the only truth or excuse I had.

"From who? Do you have friends who've had a baby recently?" she looked at me skeptically.

"A baby? Umm…" I squinted, blinking, totally confused by the conversation or brawl we were having. A baby? What did that even mean? "I—" I shook my head. "I don't follow."

She motioned to the pink cake in her mixer. "I make a lot of—" she paused, then huffed out, *"never mind.* Fine. What's your schedule like?"

"What if we figured this out at *Sherrie's*? We could have our taste-test over dinner. Friday night?" I smiled. I swooned. I charmed the crap out of that invitation.

Blake scowled at me. *"Dinner?* Did you leave your brain in the car?" And sure, maybe my timing was off—as we were just on the verge of a shouting match seconds before.

Still. *Ouch.* I coughed, gathering my confidence up from the pool of goo on the floor it had become with her reprimand. "I guess that wouldn't work."

"Uh, *nope.* I can't bake and you can't taste my cake in a restaurant." She scrolled through the screen on her computer. Huffing under her breath, she murmured, "A restaurant?" She shook her head. "How stupid?"

I cleared my throat, ignoring her cutting comments. I was on a mission, and clearly, I would hear a lot of coldness from the ice queen before I warmed her up a bit. "What about *your* schedule? When can you fit me in?"

"We need to get started soon. Would Wednesday work?"

I pulled up the calendar on my phone. Wednesday was booked

and I needed a day to talk to Fran about the cake for the Festival. I could sweet-talk Fran into this… I could. "Ahhh…"

She curled her lip and scowled. "Listen, you aren't giving me much time, I need to—"

"Right. Okay. Okay. I'll figure out Wednesday." I stared at my phone. If I moved a few things around, I could talk to Fran another day and make room for Blake on Wednesday. "Four?"

She lifted one brow and groaned. "We close at five, you'll have to be quick."

"You do want this job, right?" I shouldn't test her—she ticked like a time bomb that could go off at any moment. She was bound to say something like—*forget the whole thing* and then spend the rest of the month making potions in her covenstead.

Her jaw clenched, but her scowl left. She pursed her lips, as if holding back vile words. She touched two long, slender fingers to her brow, shooing back a few hairs that strayed from the knot on top of her head. "I do. Four it is."

CHAPTER NINE

Juliana

*J*had taken on too much. I knew I had, but how could I not? After learning that I would be designing and dressing the wedding party for Melanie Kucho's daughter's wedding, and apparently after hearing me praised by Mel—Andrea Leawood contacted me! Personally! She's rumored to be up for an Oscar next year and she wants me to design her dress for the red carpet.

After Charlotte's wedding, I'd have four months to figure out Andrea's dress. That and the smaller jobs Mark had me working on… I could do it. I could make it all work.

"Hey."

I lifted my head from the planner on my iPhone, gasping in a small breath.

Jack's brows furrowed. "Sorry—I didn't mean to startle you."

"You didn't," I said, my tone light, not overworked in the least. "Is Melanie coming?"

"She's waiting for Charlotte. I thought I'd update you on a few," he lowered his voice, conspiratorially, "Blake items."

My sister! I hadn't called her since the party. Yes, guilt filled me, but what about work? With Andrea's dress and Charlotte's wedding gown, it might be hard to find time for *anything* else. But I loved my sister. "So?"

"So, I had someone go into the bakery—another designer. He's hired her to make something for the *Cherry Blossom Festival.*"

I blinked and tilted my head. "Wow. That's great. And quick. Isn't it soon?"

"Yeah—two months. Royce just has to talk to the curator of the event and everything will be a done deal."

"I thought he hired her."

"He did," Jack said. "It's all working out. Just a little more behind-the-scenes kinks that need to be finalized."

I bit my lip. I should be helping with this more.

"I know you're meeting with Mom on Friday." His throat rose and fell with his swallow. "Would you want to have dinner after?"

Jack. *Ugh.*

He was sweet, really—and now that I paid attention, totally cute.

But between Melanie, Andrea, Dad, and Blake, I didn't know how to fit him in. I know I'd said I'd go... but he had said he'd help me even if I didn't. Right? Like he'd been telling a joke.

"I can't Friday. Besides, it's not a done deal, right? Your guy still has to talk to the people in charge. Let's wait until she's mixing cake to celebrate." I cleared my throat and stood. I could go to Melanie. She wouldn't mind. I didn't have to wait here.

"Sure," he said, his tone less chipper. He stood and before I could walk away, he reached out but didn't quite touch me. His hand hovered for a second as if not knowing where to go or what to do. "Oh, hey. Can you give us any information on Blake?"

"Information?" I didn't understand. What did he want to know?

"Yeah, just to help with this... process."

"I don't really know what you need, besides that she's a great baker." I chewed on my lip. Oh, Blake.

"Right—well, this might go a little more smoothly or success- fully if Royce could talk to her. If they became friends—sort of."

"Oh. Um, well, she…" my brain ran back to when we were kids, "she likes baseball."

"Baseball. Okay. That's helpful."

I adjusted the folders in my arms and slipped my phone into my hidden pencil skirt pocket. I crammed my eyes shut, then opened them, taking a minute. "Jack—thank you. Blake needs this and I wouldn't know how to help her on my own."

"We all need help from time to time." He looked down, his lashes fluttered as he met my gaze again. "I got you."

I licked my lips, unsure what to say. I cleared my throat, my eyes skirting around the large working room. "I'm gonna find Melanie and Charlotte."

"Sure." He gave a curt wave and shoved his fingertips into the front pockets of his chambray jeans. "I'll let you know how it's going."

I nodded, tucking a stray hair behind my ear. My heart flut- tered. *Blake.* I was a lousy sister. I should be helping her, not asking Jack to. And yet, he'd already accomplished something.

"Juliana! Come in! Come in! Charlotte is anxious to see your sketches." Melanie waved me into her glass office.

Charlotte sat, cross-legged, her long shimmering caramel hair laying in waves down her back. Her slanted eyes, traced in green and gold watched me. She never said much—always the reserved one, but I didn't doubt her intelligence. She spoke to be heard and never for noise. She was younger than Jack, by a couple years. She and Eric met in college, lost touch, and reconnected when she started at DRV Engineers.

I sat next to her, unoffended when Charlotte didn't say anything. "Hello, Charlotte. I think you'll like the changes I've made to your train." I pulled the two sketches I'd worked on for a

47

week from my folder. One showed the wedding train from the side and one straight on from the back. "I added the leavers lace here, where you asked. But I also wanted to show what it would look like over the chiffon." I pulled the next sketch from my folder.

"Oh, Juliana," Melanie said, picking up my sketch. "This is perfection. Charlotte, dearest, what are your thoughts?"

"Yes." Charlotte touched the sketch with her fingertips. Her hazel eyes, blue and brown—missing the green that Jack's held—sparkled. "This is it."

"Can you get it done in time? This is quite the change." Melanie liked me—enough to press her son on me, but when it came to Charlotte's wedding clothes, she was all business.

"It is," I smiled looking at the work I'd completed. It would be magnificent. "But I can do it."

"I know you can!" Melanie's thin lips parted into a large, beaming grin.

I smiled back, noting in the back of my mind all of the things I'd be forced to ignore to complete this job—including my father and my sister.

CHAPTER TEN

Blake

I set out the long white serving tray. I had ten little cakes in the freezer, they would be cool enough for icing soon —just in time for Royce Valentine to make his appearance. I almost vomited when he told me his last name. I thought he was lying or trying out a line on me. But he paid for the tasting—and that's what it said on his credit card. Royce D. Valentine.

Yikes.

Finally—my first tasting—for a customer, I'd done a few for job interviews. But this was a client, a big client, and they were mine.

The door jingled with my thought, the word *mine* ringing in my head just as Royce Valentine's handsome face came into view. *Gross.*

Sure, he looked good. I mean, I wasn't dead. His dark hair combed back in waves and I wondered how much time he spent making sure not a single hair sat out of place. He had to trim that short beard daily—and though I didn't normally like a beard on a man—it suited his dumb face. His topaz eyes pierced me with either eagerness… or fear—I wasn't sure.

I ignored him and his dumb eyes, pulling the cakes from the freezer. I set the small circular cakes onto my elongated tray with care.

"Are you ready for me?"

"You're early. But yes, I am ready." I'd already placed my frosting options into three ramekins. They waited, at the ready. Royce took a seat at the counter and I sat opposite of him, on the other side of the bar. My tail had just hit the seat when I stood. "Um, I'm gonna lock up." I didn't need a dumb gender reveal coming in and interrupting my tasting. I walked over to the door and flipped the lock, as well as the open sign—an hour earlier than normal. My insides fluttered and I couldn't help the small skip in my step. My first tasting!

"No one else from the festival committee wanted to be here?" I sat across from him.

His brows knit, which instantly put me on guard. "Ah, you know, they trust me."

My skeptical side rose to the surface—it tended to show its evil face pretty quick. I pushed down the emotion—this was my *first* tasting. I wouldn't let the client ruin it, no matter how chauvinistic he might be.

"Okay," I said, beaming down at my cakes. "First—"

"You have a pretty smile, Blake. You should use it more." He grinned over at me, his white teeth gleaming.

Why would he say that? "Excuse me? This is a tasting, not a self-help meeting. I don't need you telling me how to smile." I shook my head. This guy!

"Not *how*," he said, "just that you should—"

I glared, my head hot.

"Forget it." He pointed to the cakes in front of him. "You were saying?"

I cleared my throat and ground my teeth. "Yes, I was." My eyes flicked up in a roll all of their own accord. "I have ten cake flavors for you. I have suggestions for an event such as this, but I want you to try everything so you can have the final say." Although, he'd be an idiot not to go with my top choice. Somehow, I kept those words inside. It wasn't easy. What a weirdo—*you should smile more*—was he for real? "First, I'll have you try without frosting. If you like it, we'll try it with your icing of choice."

"Or with your suggested?" he said, and all at once, he seemed to take this more seriously.

"If you like." I kept cool, and I most definitely did not smile again, but my heart thumped—glad he wanted my opinion.

I pointed to each two-inch round cake atop my platter. "Almond. This is probably my top choice. It will pair nicely with the cherry-amaretto icing. Next, coconut." I showcased and titled each little cake. "Vanilla bean, chocolate, marble, red velvet, butter, butter pecan, cherry, cinnamon."

"Cinnamon?"

"It sounds weird, but it actually pairs well with cherry."

Royce rubbed his hands together and peered at my perfect little cakes. I'd baked in the back—thank goodness, where the massacre of my imperfect cake circles lay. This tray, and these beauties, spoke nothing of the mess that sat behind the baker's door.

"Time to taste?" His jaw twitched and I wondered why he'd be nervous.

"Yeah." I took a serrated knife from the counter and cut the little cake in half. I watched Royce as he brought the piece to his nose and smelled it before eating it up.

"Almond?" he said, his mouth still half full.

"Yes."

"And this is your recommendation."

"Yes, paired with the cherry-amaretto icing. You can choose though. I've prepared a cherry amaretto, chocolate, and vanilla bean."

He waved a hand, beckoning the icing onto his cake.

I slathered on the cherry-amaretto. The snow-white frosting speckled with real cherry bits had a smooth texture. I'd ground the cherry so finely that it appeared to glisten throughout the icing without discoloring or lumping it.

I watched him, chewing on my lip—it had become a bad habit. I couldn't chew on my thumbnail though, not while baking, so my lip took a beating.

His eyes closed. "Whoa."

"Whoa? What—what does that mean?" I leaned in, waiting for his answer.

He popped the rest of the little cake into his mouth. Well, I guess he wouldn't be trying another icing option with the almond. "It means, *whoa.*"

He made no sense. I knit my brows, trying to connect his dots. "And?"

"And—I know you're a fighting feminist," he raised a thumb, as if to silently say—*go feminist*—"but that was magical, you should *never* leave the kitchen." He licked his lips, his eyes finding my bowl of cherry-amaretto frosting.

"Excuse me?"

"Relax, Blake. I'm complimenting you. I've never eaten anything like that. And I've eaten a lot of fancy crap at Aunt Melanie's parties."

My lips twitched with a smirk. "*Aunt* Melanie? Melanie Kucho is your aunt?" I bust out a honking laugh, stifling it only with my hand flat to my nose and mouth. "You throw her name around like you're so special to run in her circle when you're related!" A snort snuck through my palm barricade.

He lifted one brow, his chin protruding up. "You're like a child —you know that, right?"

But he couldn't distract me with insults now. "So, you probably know her son. Right? *Jack.*"

"Um—my cousin?" he said, his tone flat. "Yes, I know my *cousin.*"

I smirked, crossing my arms. "He's half in love with my sister. Did you know that?"

He cleared his throat, seeming uncomfortable. "Yeah. I know." He rubbed a nervous hand over his forehead and down his jawline. Meeting my eyes, without even the slightest waver, he added, "I also know he's an excellent human being and she'd be an idiot not to reciprocate."

"An *idiot*? What a manly thing to say."

"I'm just saying, she couldn't do any better." He pressed his lips into a flat line and gave a small shrug.

I leaned back against the counter behind me, watching him. "Huh. I can't tell if you're lying or not."

He scoffed. "Why would I lie?"

"Oh, I don't know," I set both hands on the counter in front of me and leaned closer to him. "Because you're a MAN!"

"Geez, you're a cynical girl!" He leaned closer too—not at all intimidated. "I've never met anyone as unhappy as you Blake Minola."

We stared each other down, neither of us backing away. Royce's eyes flickered to my lips—still sneering in their purse. Then, Christian walked in from the back.

"Blake, I need you to lock up. I've got—" he stopped, taking us in.

I cleared my throat and stood straight. "We were just tasting."

Christian's eyes glanced down to the cakes on my platter. "O—kay." Christian walked around the counter, to the side where Royce stood.

Royce plopped back onto his stool.

"I've got a gender reveal coming in for you tonight. I figured you'd still be here," Christian's brows rose, "cleaning up."

My front teeth clamped down on my bottom lip, thinking of the mess I'd made in the back. "Yeah, no problem."

"See you tomorrow." He turned his attention to Royce. "Everything going well, Mr. Valentine?"

"Great," Royce gave him a toothy grin. "Couldn't be better. Blake is an amazing baker."

CHAPTER ELEVEN

Royce

*B*lake watched her boss exit out the front doors, unlocking the door she had so purposefully closed up. "Are you ready to finish the tasting?"

My teeth ground. Truthfully, I had what I wanted. She'd already given me the perfect cake. How could the committee turn me down—*again*? Now, I could tell Fran what I'd tasted—what she'd be getting. She'd have to agree this time.

Though I had the cake I wanted, I was supposed to be making friends with this shrew. For my cousin's sake, as well as the sake of my promotion, I swallowed down my temper and the tension we'd created. "What's next?"

I wanted to finish every tiny portion Blake offered me, they were all melt-in-your-mouth amazing. But the waist on my pants grew tight. I shouldn't have eaten that burrito at three. We only had three cakes left and I hadn't even gotten her talking—at least not without her sneering. Jack had said to mention baseball—which shouldn't be too difficult. I liked baseball.

She cut the little butter cake in half. "Icing or without?"

"Icing," I said, "you choose."

She slathered on more of her cherry-amaretto and handed the little cake over.

I took a drink, cleansing my palate, then popped it into my mouth, despite the tightness at my waistline. "So," I said, through a mouthful, "did you hear about Chad Kuhl?"

"Um, huh?"

"Chad Kuhl, he's the pitcher for the Rockies."

"I know who Chad Kuhl is," she said, glaring at me as if I'd asked her to loan me some money. "What about him?"

"Did you hear? He sprained his wrist. He's out for at least four weeks."

Her gaze stayed grounded, though darting left to right. She clearly did not want to react—however, she was interested. "How do you know?"

"I work with some of his people. A friend spilled the news. I think it went to the press just today."

She tapped her phone screen and nibbled on her full bottom lip. "They'll have to use Freeland on Saturday."

"Yeah, too bad."

Her brows furrowed. "Freeland should be starting."

"Serious?"

"Yes, I'm serious. His average is every bit as good as Kuhl's."

I'd piqued her interest and her bark was more curiosity than bite. "He's playing here, Saturday," I said.

The jingle above the door rang out before I could tell her about the extra ticket I wouldn't be using... And *hey*, would she want to go?

Blake's eyes slid from the counter to the door. "Eep," she gasped out and flew through the swinging door to the back kitchen.

"Uhh, what's happening?" I peeked at the couple behind me, a man and a woman, clearly expecting a baby.

56

"Hi," the woman said. "We talked to Christian. He said we could drop off our gender reveal order."

"Sure," I said, feeling a little silly. I didn't work here. "Let me grab the baker for you."

The guy scratched behind one ear, looking around the place.

I snuck back behind the counter. "Hello?" I said, pushing on the swinging door and—

"Ouch!"

I'd hit Blake.

Slipping through the door, I stared at her. "What are you doing? You have a customer and—" I stopped at her expression.

Her eyes were wide—and red. Her right thumb and her middle finger held to her opposite wrist, twisting and twisting and twisting.

She shut her eyes, clamping so hard onto her bottom lip that it turned stark white. "Neal," she whispered. I'm not even sure she knew that she'd spoken out loud.

"Neal?"

"Shh!" she hushed, waving both hands at me. With the movement, some color returned to her cheeks. She flew closer to me, facing me, only an inch of air separating the two of us. She pressed one finger to my mouth. "Don't say his name."

I breathed her in, looking down at her, seeing the honey in her irises and feeling the warmth from her near body. She smelled like sugar and sweetness. Her glistening eyes, her quivering lips, they pled with me to help her. I licked my lips, wanting for one insane second to close the gap between us.

"Go out there—pretend to be me."

My hallucination, the one where this girl wasn't whacked, ended. I blinked. "I don't follow."

She stepped back, grabbed me by the shoulders, and turned me around so that I faced the closed door. "I can't see him. Pretend to be me. Just take their stupid card and get them out!"

She pushed me, skittered back, and I found myself out front

once more. The man—*Neal*—looked annoyed, peering down at his wristwatch.

"Can... I... help... you?" I found myself saying. I was dressed in jeans and a Ralph Lauren polo. Surely they couldn't believe I worked at the bakery.

"You were getting the baker," Neal said, rubbing a hand over his shaved head.

"Ahhh," I squinted. "I'm the baker."

"But you said—"

"I'm the baker's assistant! He's—she's busy. They. Are. Busy." I cleared my throat. "I'll just take your..." What had Blake said? "*Card*? And you can go."

"Sure. We're the Huffmires," the woman rubbed her belly, small but protruding just the same. "Patricia and Neal. Can we hear our options?"

"Options?" my eyes narrowed, almost to slits.

"Flavors?"

"Sure," I looked at the almost empty plate of mini cakes Blake had baked for me. "You've got your traditional vanilla. Your chocolate. Your vanilla with little chopped nuts in it. Umm... the almond! Whew, that's a fan favorite. I can tell you from experience, it's to die for."

The pretty girl smiled. "Let's go with that. *Almond*. We'd like it frosted half pink, half blue."

I looked at the counter for a paper and pen. Nothing. The couple watched me. I tapped my head. "Got it. Not to worry." I glanced back at the closed kitchen door. "We're closing up though. You gotta go."

"But the deposit—"

"Pay later. It's fine." I walked out from behind the counter and waved my hands, sweeping them out the door like I would a pesky, unwelcome cat. I shut the glass door behind them and turned the latch on the lock. Breathing out, I looked up to meet the couple still looking through the window, watching me. I waved once more, sending them on their way.

I trudged back to the counter, running a hand through my hair. What in the world was that? "They're gone!" I watched the swinging door. Nothing. "Hey, Blake!" I said. "They've gone!"

Making my way to the back, I smacked the door open, this time not really caring if it bumped into her. She'd put me in an awkward position. I looked like an idiot out there. I peered around the large, industrial kitchen. The extra cake she'd made sat in heaps of discarded circles on one counter. Dirty bowls and mixing utensils piled high in the sink. But I didn't see Blake.

Until—I heard her. Her muffled sob came from a back corner. My heart pattered in my chest, unsure of what'd I'd find and totally baffled at what I should do. "Blake?" I said again, this time soft.

She sat on the ground, her hair out of its pins, lay in long strings down her back. Her knees drew up to her chest and she wrapped both her arms around them. Her forehead pressed against her knees and her back shook with sobs.

I watched her, heart racing, with no clue what to say or do. My initial thought—*this girl has issues.* But more than that, I could see she suffered. Neal something-or-other had caused this agony.

"Blake?" I said quietly.

Her hold on her legs tightened, but she didn't lift her head. I wouldn't kneel down by her—I didn't think she'd want that. Not to mention she might bite my head off, *literally.* But I couldn't leave either.

I ran a hand through my hair and peered about the large kitchen again. Three rows of silver counters ran the length of the kitchen, each with a sink, stove, and baking equipment, one sat covered in the preparation disaster of my tasting.

My loafers tapped on the tile floor, as I walked to the sink with multiple dirty mixing bowls in it. I rolled up my sleeves and turned on the hot water. Searching, I found some soap, then began to wash.

~

Two hours later, Blake's kitchen sat sparkling clean. I picked up the bakery box I'd found in a closet—I'd filled it with half the leftovers of Blake's almond cake circles—and walked over to where Blake still sat. I cleared my throat and rocked on my heels. "Hey Blake," I said, and my voice seemed to vibrate off the walls of the large room.

She lifted her head. Her hair, cheeks, and knees were wet from the endless tears that attempted to drown her. She sniffed. Her face had gone a blotchy red and her eyes had swelled with her cries.

I swallowed, saddened at the sight of this feisty girl dashed to pieces. "I'm going to go. I'm taking the leftovers from that almond cake—if that's okay."

She didn't answer, only looked at me with eyebrows squished together.

"I think the committee will love it. I wanted them to try it. It really is amazing. And your opinion was spot on. Almond with the cherry-amaretto it is. We can talk design next time I see you."

Still, she didn't speak. I nodded a little her way, my mouth closed in a tight-lipped grin. What else could I do? I'd cleaned the kitchen, leaving a neat stack of the dishes I couldn't see a space for. I'd packed up the cake and left her all but the almond.

Her eyes, bright from her tears looked like honey, newly harvested.

"Well, see you," I said when she didn't say anything back. I turned and left her alone, wondering who Neal was, wondering how he'd turned the saltiest girl I'd ever met into a pile of mush.

CHAPTER TWELVE

Jack

I'd never been to Juliana's work before—I'd never hunted her down before—at least, outside of Mom's work or one of her parties. Sure, Mom always shot me a text when Juliana arrived, but I wanted to know. I didn't stop her.

I pulled up to the brick building on California Street. The large windows facing the street told me the building stood six floors high. I just needed to know which floor Juliana worked on. I couldn't ask Mom—not when I came here on a secret mission. I just hoped there would be a directory once inside.

I stepped inside and unlike *The Creative Drive*, this place had offices with walls and closed doors. Luckily, a girl sat at a desk made of a glass top and mahogany wooden legs. She set her corded phone back on its receiver just as I entered.

"Can I help you?"

I pretended to know my way around. I acted as if I was supposed to be there—and not what it truly was—me surprising Juliana at work. "I'm here to see Juliana Minola."

"Third floor. Elevator's to the left." She motioned with a point, then picked her phone back up.

Well, that was easy enough. I found the elevator just as easily and, with my heart thudding, rode it to the third floor. I wished for once in my life I could be a normal guy, that I could be like Royce, and just turn all the nerves off.

But as often as I told my head to chill out and my heart to calm down, when it came to Juliana, my body had a mind of its own.

Another glass and mahogany desk with another girl with a phone. She set hers down, much like the first had, and I realized that if someone were to line the two up, I wouldn't know which sat on the first floor and which sat on the third floor. I didn't see other women—just Juliana. I'd never had that experience before.

"Hi," she said, "here for Ms. Minola?"

"I am."

The first-floor girl must have called the third floor because there were several offices with a variety of names on doors on this floor.

She gave me a sideways look. "Is she expecting you?" And the way she said it told me she knew that Juliana had no idea I waited out here.

"Oh. Well, no. But she'll want to see me."

"Will she now?" She grinned—forced and false. "Your name?"

"Jack. Anderson. Jack Anderson." I shoved my nervous hands into my pockets, hoping the sweat sliding down my back didn't show through the button-up dress shirt I wore.

She scrunched her nose at me, condescendingly, and stood from her seat. She walked to the second door on the right, tapped, then poked her head into the office.

I waited, watching, hoping Juliana wouldn't send me away. But then, maybe she had a client. Maybe she had a strict schedule and couldn't be interrupted. She was overworked—I knew that without a doubt.

The girl walked back to her desk—her strut less forced. She lifted one brow, looking me over. Forcing another smile, one too big for her face, she said, "You can go in."

My broad shoulders, strong from swimming competitively for ten years, straightened. I peered at her—hopefully seeming not surprised at all. "Thanks," I said, making my way to the door she'd poked her head inside.

Before I could make it the entire length of the carpet, Juliana opened the door, greeting me. "Jack. What are you doing here?" Her soft smile blossomed in that kind way of hers. She didn't seem annoyed at my arrival.

"I wanted to see you," I said—stupidly. "And talk about," I peered behind me, "Blake," I said in a hushed tone.

Juliana beckoned me inside and shut the door.

"Maybe we need a code word."

Her brows knit in question.

"You know for when we need to talk…" I shrugged. "We could call it Mission Cake Boss."

"Jack," she shook her head. "I don't think that's necessary."

I shrugged one shoulder. She hadn't laughed or agreed. I sounded like a ten-year-old. That's fine—it was *just* Juliana, *just* the girl of my dreams. Who cared if I made a fool of myself?

"Come in. Sit down. What's up?" Her eyes squinted with a grin, but she glanced at her phone screen for half a second before meeting me eye to eye once more.

I sat in one of two chairs on the other side of her desk. Juliana was organized, but she had a lot of files and catalogs sitting atop her desk—*overworked*, I knew it! I swallowed. "Well, Royce had his tasting with Blake."

"Great." Another glance at her smartphone. "How did it go?"

"Good—mostly. He said she mentioned a *Neal*, although he doesn't have any information on him, only that Blake mentioned his name. Can you tell us more?"

She set her phone down on the desk. "She told him about Neal?" She sunk into the chair next to me, giving me her full attention.

"No. Not at all, actually. I guess he came into the shop."

Juliana sucked in a breath and cupped a hand around her mouth. Her eyes stared at me like laser beams. "What did he say to her?"

"Oh." I ran a hand through my hair. Clearly, this guy meant something to Juliana as well. "Nothing. She ran to the back. He only spoke to Royce."

Sinking back into the plush pink chair, Juliana sighed. "Oh, Blake." She bit down on her thumbnail and whispered to herself, "Why would he go into the shop? The jerk never once stepped into her workplace before. I'm not even sure he knew the name of it."

"Juliana, who is he?"

She blinked, whisps of tears clinging to her long eyelashes. "Once upon a time, he was Blake's fiancé."

"Oh." My eyes widened. Neither Royce nor I could imagine Blake engaged—he'd encountered her a lot more than I had, but even with the little interaction I'd had, she didn't seem like the kind of girl who'd want to get married.

"Yeah. You're surprised. Well, the last year and a half has changed my sister. I mean, she's still her, but a much less happy version." Juliana sniffed.

I set a hand on her knee. "That's what we're trying to change. Right?"

She nodded, pinching her lips and glancing over at me. "Right."

The phone atop her desk buzzed and she blinked. She snatched it up and peered at the screen. Licking her lips, she said, "Anything else?"

My brows drew together—I liked Juliana, but I didn't always understand her. I knew she cared about her sister, but she also didn't seem to have *time* to care about her sister. "Yeah. Royce got tickets to the Rockies game on Saturday." I held the two out to her.

She stared at them, then a nervous laugh bubbled in her throat. "Umm?" She shook her head, not understanding.

"For you and Blake. It'll put her in a good mood. She likes baseball."

Juliana let out a breathy laugh, still not taking the tickets. "Yes. But—but I can't take her to the game. I mean, give her the tickets."

"And who would she go with? Juliana, she doesn't have any friends." At least it seemed that way. "She has *you*." I peered at her, sternly, not caring that I hoped to impress her and win her over. My integrity wouldn't let me care.

She drooped her head to the side. "And I have a meeting with your mother and Charlotte."

"It's a *Saturday*. You need a day off."

"I have days off."

"No." I shook my head. "You don't."

"Well, I..." she stammered, crossing her legs, then uncrossing them. Finally, she stood and walked around the desk to her office chair. "I don't like days off."

I sputtered an unhumorous laugh. "That's not true."

She tipped her head back, staring at the ceiling. "Fine. But I don't have time for a day off. Not right now."

"Juliana, have you always been this selfish?" I felt the truth of my words, but I regretted saying them the minute they came out.

"Selfish?" Her eyes widened. "You think I'm selfish?"

I didn't say anything. I couldn't.

"Why in the world would you want to spend an evening out with such a selfish person, Jack?"

I rubbed the space between my bottom lip and my chin. "Juliana, you are one of the most talented, elegant, graceful people I know. You have ideas that have changed people. You make average things beautiful. You're special. And I know that. And I do want to go out with you."

She harumphed and crossed her arms, not meeting my eyes.

I set the tickets to the game on top of her desk and stood.

Walking to the door, I glanced back. "Your sister needs you, Juliana. I'm trying. Royce is trying. But you're her family."

CHAPTER THIRTEEN

Juliana

I couldn't believe Jack Anderson had spoken to me that way. He'd called me selfish. I'm *not* selfish. I work sixty hours a week. Mark trusts me with new projects and instead of passing them off to others, even when I don't have the time, I say yes.

I loved my sister. How many tears had I shed on Blake's behalf—more than Jack Anderson could count, that was for sure.

So, why did I feel so wretchedly guilty? Why did my heart break every time the broken record in my head played his words over and over again? *I'm trying, but you're her family*, he'd said. I blinked back the tears and chewed on my right thumbnail, my heart thumping in what felt like strange irregular beats.

My office phone buzzed and I picked up the receiver, not a quiver in my tone, "Yes, Kasey?"

"Mark would like to see you in his office."

"Thank you." I breathed in, blew out the breath, and counted to ten. I was at work. I would compose myself. I would not fall apart.

I stood, my calves feeling the six-inch heels I wore. I'd already put in eight hours today. I walked to the back of the floor to Mark Zudora's nine-hundred square foot office.

I knocked once and waited for his—

"Enter."

I stepped inside to Mark's oasis at work. Mark stood in front of a drawing board, sketching a man's suit, a coat long with tails. He gave one more touch to the drawing before turning to face me. His dark eyes smiled when he saw me.

"Juliana, did I ever tell you congrats on the Andrea Leawood job? I'm so proud of you." He tucked one of the straying dreadlocks tied into a knot at the back of his head back into place. Mark may have been twenty years my senior, but his soul would be forever young.

"You did, *twice*," I chuckled. "But thank you."

"I'm just so proud of you. The Kucho job and now this. You're going places, girl."

"I appreciate that, Mark. It means a lot coming from you." While Melanie was the only woman in the top ten for web designers, Mark was the first African American in the western states to win the CDFA award for his insanely creative and fashion-forward brain. I was literally surrounded by legends.

"You deserve every bit of my praise, Juliana. You're the first one here in the morning and the last one here at night. You're making it because you're working for it." He smiled and his white seemed to shine.

"I don't know if you're interested, but I just had another call —*for you*."

I swallowed, blinking too many times, and tied my hands in a knot at my front so I wouldn't chew off a thumbnail in front of Mark Zudora. "Oh, yeah? Who?"

Mark laughed. "She says so nonchalantly."

"Well?" I said, my heart pounding.

"Amy Allen."

"Eep." My hand went to my mouth. "The country singer?"

"You're all the rage, Juliana."

I nibbled on my lip—something Blake would have done.

Blake. My sister. I cleared my throat. I hardly had time to see her now. "Can I think about it, Mark?"

He chuckled. "You know you're an *"it"* girl when you're picking and choosing jobs." He winked at me. "I know you've got a lot on your plate right now. "Take twenty-four hours."

~

I reread my text to Jack Anderson, then hit send.

```
Distract your mother this afternoon, so she
  doesn't sit and stew about how much she
                loathes me.
```

His reply came quick:

```
        Why would she ever do that?
```

I puffed out my cheeks and typed back:

```
Because I rescheduled our meeting today to take
        my sister to a baseball game.
```

He sent back an incredibly unprofessional GIF of a hippopotamus doing a happy dance. I stifled a laugh. Why did I tell him anyway? Why did I care if Jack Anderson thought me selfish or not? I knew that I loved my sister and father. I knew that I did all I could for them—even if that meant I didn't see them as often as Jack Anderson thought I should. He didn't know me *that* well.

Still, I'd sent the text... so the logical part of my brain told me that I didn't want Jack believing me a selfish person. Because I'm not. But juggling work and family right now—especially with Blake in this... *funk*—it had all become so complicated. Dad understood when it took me a few days to call him back and even longer to stop by. He knew how hard I'd been working. He was proud of me. But Blake... she didn't notice, or care, she only felt her own bitterness.

I believed Jack could help though. The *Cherry Festival* job was a big deal—that had to boost her spirits. This would be the new start she needed.

I tapped on her apartment door, knowing she wouldn't answer, knowing she still wore her Bart Simpson pajama pants—the ones I would truly love to burn—eating something weird for breakfast like cheese puffs or ice cream. At 11:30 a.m., I hoped she'd been up for maybe an hour—if not, it would be difficult to get her moving.

Key at the ready, I unlocked the door and made my way inside Blake's downtown apartment. Her little living room-kitchen combo sat empty with stinky dishes in the sink. I could hear Homer Simpson's dull voice sound from Blake's bedroom.

I stormed down the hall—on a mission, now that I'd taken the time to come. I stopped in the doorway. She lay atop her bed—in her PJ pants and faded Cherry Creek High School T-shirt—just as I'd predicted. She watched the Simpsons, a Tupperware container filled with Doritos and Swedish Fish in her hands. She stabbed at a chip with her spoon, broke it into pieces, then spooned it and a fish into her mouth.

"Ew." I adjusted the baseball cap on my head and crossed my arms, staring at her.

"What are you doing here and why are you dressed like a little boy?" She sounded bored, she didn't move from her spot, but her eyes left Bart for me.

I looked down at my Babe Ruth T-shirt, tucked into my skinny stonewashed Levi's.

She turned her attention back to the television. "You've already been here this month."

I swallowed down the guilt that sentence triggered and picked up her remote. "You are a freaking mess, Blake. Get out of bed and eat some real food." I turned the TV off—that got her attention more than my mini outburst.

"Hey!" she moaned. "I was watching that."

"No, you were sitting here wasting away your day." I would not cancel on Melanie Kucho, just to have Blake turn me down. "I have tickets." I pulled the two Rockies tickets from my pocket and flapped them a foot in front of her face. "So, get up."

Her brows knit and she looked at me as if I'd grown an extra head. "You don't like baseball."

"No." I set my hands on my hips. "But *you* do. And I had a client give these to me."

She looked at the tickets clutched in my hand at my hip. She grunted and rolled away from me. "Take Dad."

"I'm taking *you*."

She moaned. "It's my day off, Juliana."

"And going to a baseball game is so taxing!" I slapped her behind, right on Bart's face.

She yelped and jerked.

So, I slapped her bottom again. "Come on! Time to get up!" One more time—slapping Blake's butt was somehow liberating. "Don't make me dress you again."

"Fine!" she barked. She rolled off the bed, onto her knees, and on the floor, then looked up at me. "I'm up. Okay?"

"Great!" A pair of jeans dangled over her desk chair, I picked them up and threw them at her. "Now, get dressed. I don't want to miss the opening pitch."

71

CHAPTER FOURTEEN

Blake

I loved Coors Field in Denver. Sure, it was tough at times being a Rockies fan, but the field always made me feel lighter on the inside somehow. The trees surrounding the space were vast and each so different. I loved the Navajo sandstone and the marble boulders, too, but especially the fountain, right at center field. And when the Rockies hit a home run the small spurts of water jutting up from the ground would shoot out, reaching forty feet into the sky. When we were kids, Dad would get us seats right next to the fountain. The Rockies would score or win and water would spurt up from the ground, and mists from the explosion would fall onto my face, kissing my cheeks and head.

I hadn't looked at Juliana's tickets, so I had no idea where we'd be sitting today. I followed her, not ready to talk just yet. It had been a rough weekend after seeing Neal. I didn't want to leave my bed. But Jewels had been right. I needed to get out. I cringed at the thought of myself lying in bed, pouting because of Neal Huffmire.

I followed after Juliana, right behind home plate—just out of reach of the fountain mist. Still, good seats—great seats, in fact. Field level, third row? These were pretty fantastic seats.

"Where did you say you got these tickets?"

"A client," she said, looking down at the numbers on the seats. "You're here." She tapped the seat just beside her and sat on the one next to it.

I breathed in the April air. The beautiful spring day had already reached sixty-two degrees. The sun shone high, with minimal clouds. The smell of popcorn and corndogs wafted in the air and I couldn't feel totally miserable—even if I tried.

"How's work?" she said, watching the field.

I gave her a sideways glance. "Why?"

"Just a question, Blake."

I bit my inner cheek. "Not... *terrible.*"

"*Really?*" Juliana turned in her seat. "And why is that? Are you starting to love gender reveals?"

I coughed out a laugh. "Um, *no.*"

"Did you find a new way to sabotage people's orders?"

This time I didn't cough—I just laughed. "Not yet. But I'm working on it." I stirred in my seat. It felt strange bragging about my new job to Juliana who designed gowns for movie stars and multimillionaires. "I got a pretty cool assignment, though."

"Yeah?"

"The *Cherry Blossom Festival.* You know, for the city? They want me to be in charge of the main dessert for the event." I nibbled at the loose skin on my bottom lip, my heart thumping annoyingly in my chest. It sounded so lame.

"Blake, that's big." She grinned at me. She made it sound wonderful. "You know that, right?" She looked at me, pride in her eyes. The shock I'd feared wasn't there. But then, she believed I could do something like this—even before I believed it.

My mouth turned up in a grin. I'm not sure I could have suppressed it. "Yeah. I know."

"Well, congrats. Consider this our celebration."

"No way. You can't say the gift you've already given me is for this new accomplishment you just learned about."

She rolled her eyes playfully. "Fine!"

"No, you have to get me something else." I nodded, as if it were the law. "Something pretty fabulous. Something that tops these seats."

She laughed. "Blake—you're joking! You!" She pointed at me, making me feel all weird about something that two years ago would have been perfectly normal.

I set a hand to her cheek, then shoved her gaze back to the field. "Stop looking at me like that."

"Fine!" She giggled. "Fine. Sorry." We quieted, watching the field and the growing crowd.

Soon the players were on the grass and the announcer asked us to rise for the National Anthem. My insides bubbled with childhood giddiness. I stood, held my hand to my heart, and watched the huge American flag fly in the wind.

"Play ball!"

CHAPTER FIFTEEN

Royce

I sat a dozen rows up from Blake and Juliana. Close enough to watch her and far enough away to be unde-tected. It wasn't creepy—it was research.

She seemed to be having fun—mostly. At least she wasn't yelling at anyone and she wasn't scowling the entire time. She watched the game with intensity, standing through half of it. She even hip-bumped Juliana once, spilling her sister's popcorn down the front of her, and then laughed her can off. I sniggered too. It was nice—seeing her this way, playful and fun. You know, as a human being.

She stood once more. Her jeans, faded and tight, fit her just right. And... she would have punched me in the gut for that thought. It may have been deserved. She waved at the vendor walking the stands selling bags of popcorn.

I darted a glance his way, but he wasn't looking at her.

"Hey!" I heard Blake roar—even a dozen rows up. "Popcorn guy!"

Juliana tugged on her sister's shirt, trying to make her sit, giving the people behind them apologetic glances.

Still, Blake stood her ground, then hopped up and down waving at the guy. He started her way and she turned to her sister. I could see her mouth move, her long chestnut brown hair waving with the breeze. She looked as if she scolded Juliana, then shrugged her shoulders, bought a bag of popcorn, and handed it to her sister.

I sat back in my stadium seat, a hand covering the smile on my face. This interesting girl had my attention. She exuded so much anger... but was it real or a shield? She was cynical but funny. She growled at everyone—including her family, but she clearly loved her sister.

I watched as her hand dug into Juliana's new bag of popcorn and then suddenly, corn in hand she pointed at the field. I looked out at the game I'd been ignoring, to see Helton running the bases, his newly hit ball nowhere in sight. The crowd shot to their feet, I peered around the guys in front of me, finding Blake as she jumped for joy, shaking Juliana and knocking the new bag of popcorn out of her sister's hands. Her head rolled back with laughter that I couldn't hear and for the strangest reason—I really wanted to hear that laugh.

My phone in my pocket buzzed. I looked at my smartwatch, at the call I'd be ignoring. *Fran.* Nope, I couldn't ignore this—not if I planned to secure Blake this job.

I pulled my phone from my pocket and answered the call. "Hey! Fran, thanks for calling!" With one finger in my ear, I made my way across the row of roaring fans, looking for a quiet spot. Did that exist at a ballgame?

I glanced back at Blake, who, along with the crowd, sang, *Take Me Out to the Ball Game*, before returning my attention to the phone.

"You said it was urgent."

"Yeah. Did you try that cake I sent over?" I'd delivered Blake's almond cake to Fran's office the day following our tasting.

"I did."

"And those were just her leftover pieces, the parts she didn't use —I mean, this girl is the real deal." I sold Blake—or at least I tried. I'd tasted the proof, she'd earned my endorsement.

"Is this your sister, Royce? Or a new client? Why are you pushing this?"

I forced a laugh. "No, not a client or a relative. I just have a feeling this is exactly what the festival needs."

"That's not really your job," she said.

"I know. And you're right. But I find myself very invested in the festival and I'd like to help."

Fran sighed. "Help by setting up booths with us the night before, Royce. We always need help with setup. *The food is planned.* It's been planned for months."

"You could add this in—it would literally be icing on the *Cherry Festival* cake." I laughed, trying to sound smooth, but my normal coolness was gone. I felt desperate, but not for me, for Blake. I could not go back to this girl and tell her the deal was off. Especially after Jack had explained to me about Neal. I couldn't do it. I wouldn't do it.

"The budget is spent." Fran's tone told me she wouldn't be budging on this topic.

I crammed my eyes closed. "Ahh—" I tapped my foot spastically on the ground. "I'll pay for it. My treat for my favorite client."

Fran paused on the other end. "*You* want to pay for it?"

I puffed out my cheeks—not really, but I didn't see how to move forward with plan—*turn-Blake-back-into-a-real-girl* without this job. It would fail otherwise. Not to mention I'd lose my promotion. "I do. As long as you'll have a place to display it." I stilled waiting for her answer.

"Fine." She groaned. "Whatever. Just make sure you do your actual job and have the links working on our website."

"Already done," I said, thankful I'd corrected the tweaks on the festival's site this morning. I hung up the phone and sighed. How much would a three-tiered cake from Blake set me back?

I started for my seat, peering back down to where I knew Blake would be. She stood next to an empty seat, her body swaying, though the crowd had stopped singing. Juliana must have gone for food or the bathroom.

Gritting my teeth, I continued downward, past my assigned seat and onto Blake's row. I had no plan, but I wanted to see her good spirits closer up. I made my excuses, moving through the people seated in her row until I got to Juliana's empty seat.

I stopped, standing next to her.

She stared out at the field. "You better not have bought diet. You *know* I hate diet. If you're going to die because of your drink, Juliana, you might as well be drinking the real thing."

I guffawed and she started, her head whipping around to me. "I didn't bring diet—but then, I didn't bring a drink at all. After that speech though, I'm not sure which is worse."

She turned back to the game, acting as if she weren't surprised to see me at all. "You probably do drink diet." She made a face. "Or worse, Dr. Pepper."

I laughed and she glanced over at me, biting her lip—I think to keep from smiling.

"You're not surprised to see me here?" I asked.

She lifted one shoulder. "It's a big stadium." She peered at me again. "I mean, I didn't exactly *expect* you to show up in my sister's seat."

It was actually my seat, mine plus one. I had to buy another ticket to be there at all after giving the tickets to Jack. "Yeah, well, I saw you down here, alone."

"I'm not alone," she was quick to say. "My sister's here."

I nodded. "Enjoying the game?"

"Sure," she said, as if she didn't care. But I could see in her face she enjoyed it. She talked as if the other day never happened, like I didn't see her crying and distraught on the ground, and I pretended too.

I needed to ask this girl out—and now, when she wasn't totally miserable might be the best time. "Blake," I said, my tone charming.

"What?" she barked, in a pitch that said the opposite of charming and friendly.

Clearing my throat, I adjusted the cap on my head. *Just jump in, Royce,* I told myself. Just like the deep end at the city pool. "I'd love to take you to dinner tomorrow."

I purposely didn't form a question. No question, no rejection.

Her brows knit together and she studied me as if a horn grew from my head. "Why?"

"I like talking to you."

Her face scrunched. "No. You don't."

"If I didn't, why would I come down here? Why would I ask you to dinner?" I said, my patience slipping.

"I'm pretty sure to prove you can get any girl, any time."

I flapped my hands at my side. "Who am I trying to prove that to? You, my feminist friend?"

"What's wrong with feminism?"

"Nothing." I drooped, tired already. "Girl power." I held up one fist, but my tone dragged with the fight that I always had to bring when talking to Blake.

She smirked. "Saying *girl power* doesn't make you an advocate for women."

With my cheeks puffed, I blew out a sigh. "I just asked you to dinner."

"When a man asks a woman out, it makes him a man. But if a woman does it, it makes her domineering."

"Seriously Blake, I don't know how this conversation got so turned around. If you'd like to ask me out, I won't call you domineering. I'll just say yes." I bent forward with my last words, pushing them out with another exasperated sigh.

79

"But that's just it—you *didn't* ask me, did you? You said *you'd love to take me to dinner*, and I'm what—supposed to fall at your feet thanking you for the opportunity?"

The guy in front of us spun around. "Hey there, watching the game, here. Maybe you should try it." His pale face had gone red—our conversation clearly disturbing him.

"Mind your own business!" Blake snapped, at the same time I scowled and growled out, "Then turn around and watch!"

He thrust his hand holding his drink downward, sloshing it onto the couple in front of him. "Argh. I'm—I'm sorry. So sorry." He ignored us, too busy making amends.

I leaned closer to her and hissed in her ear. "I'm not sure how you turned a simple dinner invitation into an offensive statement. But just for the record—I wasn't trying to offend you. I was asking you to dinner. If you're ever hungry and you don't feel like ripping into anyone, let me know. The offer still stands."

I shoved my hands into my pockets, just as C.J. Cron cracked the ball with his bat. The crowd around us started to sing—*Take me out to the ball game, take me out to the fair*—and I sang along, inching my way out of Blake's row.

CHAPTER SIXTEEN

Blake

"*W*ho was that?" Juliana handed me a cola and sat, sipping on her own, only diet.

"Uh," I dipped my head and glanced back the way Royce had gone. Though, I couldn't see him amongst the sea of people. I hoped he didn't see me looking for him. "Just a client." He'd surprised me with his visit, but even more so with his dinner invitation. Of course, I wouldn't go with him, we were never in the same room without arguing. Although... he wasn't totally terrible. He'd done the dishes for me after I had a mental breakdown and cried in front of him, and he never mentioned the incident. The thought still horrified me. And in his baseball cap and under the sunshine, his eyes seemed to brighten with a playfulness I hadn't noticed before.

"A gender reveal?"

I scoffed, imagining Royce becoming a father. "No! He's over the dessert for the *Cherry Festival*."

"Oh." Her eyes went wide. "OH!" Her smile broadened, looking too joyful. "Your big account! So exciting."

"Oh, yeah! And guess who he's related to?

Her brows rose, asking without words.

"Your client—Melanie Kucho."

In the middle of a drink, Juliana coughed and sputtered on her diet soda. "No way," she said through fits of trying to breathe.

I studied her. "Yep." I tilted my head to the side, still watching her. "What's wrong with you?"

Juliana pounded on her chest. "Just swallowed wrong."

I snagged a kernel of her popcorn and tossed it into my mouth. "And," I said, needing to say the bizarre truth out loud, "he asked me out." I kept my eyes on the game, I didn't want to see her reaction.

Another fit of coughing let loose from my sister.

"What is your problem? Did you forget how to drink?" I wiped her spittle from my arm.

"No—I'm… I'm…" she shrugged, wiping her face with a napkin. "I'm surprised, okay?"

My mouth went tight as if tasting something bad. "Shocker, right?"

Juliana rolled her eyes—as if she were in middle school. "Oh, geez, Blake. I didn't mean I was surprised someone asked you out." She smacked my shoulder, looking down on me—of course. At five feet ten inches, she stood four inches taller than me. "Just that you'd allow someone close enough to let them."

"I can't decide if that should offend me more or not."

"Well, don't choose to be offended by facts." She full-on faced me now. "Come on, Blake. You know as well as I do, you've pretty much shut off the world this past year and a half."

I licked my lips, but my throat had gone dry and it didn't help. I downed a swig of my cola, squinting out at the green field and players that had become dots. She wasn't wrong. But I didn't want to give Neal credit for the way I behaved—good or bad.

Juliana slid an arm around my shoulders. "Is he cute?" she said, her tone changed from lecturing to intrigued.

"He…" I said, a picture of Royce popping into my brain. "He isn't not cute."

Juliana laughed. "I don't know what that means."

"I don't know!" I shrugged dramatically, but her arm didn't budge from around me. "He's got this hair," I motioned my hand over my head. "It's dark and kind of wavy. And his eyes are really dark—but this weird shade of brown too. Like topaz. Sometimes he wears glasses—they're kind of round and marbled. And I don't know why, but I like them on his face. They make him look slightly less conceited."

Juliana's shoulders shook with a silent laugh. "You *like* him."

I slapped her arm from my shoulder. "I do not." Was she stupid? I did not like Royce Valentine. I didn't even know him, except that he, more often than not, annoyed me. "He's cocky and pompous. He knows how wonderful he is—believe me."

She stared to the right and slightly down, meeting my eyes dead on and making me a little uncomfortable. Still, I never backed down from a fight. "You called his eyes *topaz*."

"So?"

"You don't call some random guy's eyes *topaz*. You call them brown."

"If you say I like him again, I'm leaving."

"Before 7th inning?"

"I'm serious, Juliana!"

She snaked her arm back around my shoulders, rocking us side to side. "*Take me out to the ballgame…*" she sang.

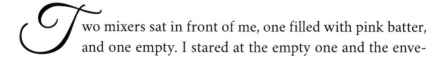

wo mixers sat in front of me, one filled with pink batter, and one empty. I stared at the empty one and the enve-

lope beside it. I hadn't opened it yet. It belonged to Neal and I just
—I couldn't.

I chewed on my bottom lip, the envelope taunting me, when
the bell above the shop door rang.

Royce.

My insides jumped like bouncy balls had been dumped in
through a hole in my head. This was all Juliana's fault. I schooled
my expression, barely glancing at him, before looking back down
at my mixing cake. I picked up my dye and toothpick and slathered
in another unneeded clump of fuchsia dye.

"Hey," he said, walking toward me.

The front had two counters, one against the wall and one the
customers could reach, I stood between them, like jelly in a sandwich. My mixers sat on the back counter, for sanitary reasons—
out of the reach of others.

Still, Royce lifted his eyes, looking inside both of my mixers.
"What are you making?"

I bobbed my head like a valley girl in the movie Clueless.
"Gender reveals," I said, my tone high and sickly sweet.

He chuckled. "Sounds fun."

"Meh." It wasn't horrible—not with the game I played. Today
the Johnsons would get the news that a baby girl would soon be
joining their family. Only… a *he* would soon be born, not a she.

His brows knit, and he pushed up on the rim of his marbled
glasses. "Doesn't that card say boy?"

I gave him an obnoxious blaring grin. "Congrats! You passed
first grade!"

"But your cake—"

"Yes, my cake is pink." I rolled my eyes—I wasn't afraid to tell
him about my game—because, *guess what, Juliana,* I didn't care
what he thought of me! "I like to play, *guess the gender* with myself.
So, I guess, then I make the cake. Sometimes I'm right, sometimes
I'm wrong."

To my shock, Royce doubled over in laughter. He stood straight, wiping at a tear forming in his right eye. "That's the best."

I bit my lip, keeping my smile in check. "It's entertaining for a job I dislike."

"I bet," he said. He sat, only using an inch or two of my unused counter as his seat, still looking at my mixing bowls. "Don't you get any complaints?"

I chewed on my cheek. I had never discussed this with anyone but Juliana and she didn't have questions, she just thought me awful. "Not as many as you'd think." I shrugged one shoulder and turned off the mixer with the pink batter. "I think most people are corrected by their doctors if they have a second ultrasound. Those that don't are in love with the kid that comes and by then they're too busy and don't care. Some assume the doctor misread the ultrasound or that they wrote it down incorrectly. A few... complain." I swallowed. "But Christian is pretty sure there is one doctor in the Denver area who can't read a sonogram to save his life. I'm the only one who sees what's written on the card... so, how can they dispute?"

"But the doctor writes it. He sees it."

"He does. But we had a couple tell us their doctor apologized, he's overworked and sees so many women in a week, he honestly couldn't remember what he had written."

"Wow, Blake Minola, making gynecologists look sheepish all over the city."

I laughed. I couldn't help it. I pinched my lips shut as if I'd said something I regretted rather than laughed at his joke.

"Your cake is so delicious, they probably forget to complain."

I cleared my throat with his compliment.

"What's your guess for that one?" He pointed to Neal's sealed envelope.

I looked down into my pink batter, the bright bubble gum color turned fuchsia. "Um. I don't know." I picked up the card for the Mackeys, clearly marked BOY, and tapped it on the metal counter. Then glanced at the envelope I'd yet to open. "That's Neal's card." I shook my head. But Royce had seen me cry... in a *corner*... on the *ground*. So, I knew it wouldn't be a shock that it made me uncomfortable.

"Oh," he said, sliding himself from the counter and standing on both feet. "That's... weird."

"Yeah. That's what it is. *Weird*." Weird sounded better than the way I felt inside. *Pathetic*. Neal's cake was due today. I should have baked it yesterday. "I just need to get it done." With Royce there to distract me, I started on auto-mode. He jabbered on about the festival cake and I combined and blended, until a white batter mixed in my once empty bowl.

When I'd done all I could, he stopped his small talk chatter and walked around to where I stood, on the other side of the counter. "How about I look? You don't have to know. This could be just another forgettable cake."

I met his eyes—*topaz* and bright. Then, I reached for the envelope and handed it over to him.

"Just another cake," I said.

"Yep. Which means you take your guess. You might be right. You might not."

I nodded. He was right. No sabotage. Just another cake.

"So, you wanna tell me who Neal is?"

"Nope." I ground my teeth, and with my eyes closed, I snagged one of my two dyes sitting on the counter. Pink. "Girl it is," I said, looking over at him.

"I mean, I have my suspicions about the guy," he said, not dropping the subject.

I dipped into the bright blushing pink with a toothpick and lobbed it into the white batter. Heart pounding, my mouth began without permission. "Neal and I were engaged until he met Patricia—our florist. He left me for her and they've been married about a year now." I peeked over at him, trying to sound uncaring. "I'm not exactly sure. I wasn't invited to the wedding." However, my non-caring coolness died when I smacked the mixer on—a level or three too high—and pink and white batter splattered onto my apron, as well as Royce's clean blue polo.

I switched the lever down, shutting off my mixer. "Crap. I'm sorry!" I snatched a rag and wiped at his shirt, a stream of pink ran down the blue fabric. "Crap. That's going to stain."

He peered down at me and that's when I smelled him. Cucumber and mint. I shook my head—why did I notice that?

I pressed my lips in on one another. "Quick, give me your shirt."

"Aww—" he looked down at the rosy mark spreading out across the fabric.

I waved my fingers, asking for his clothes. He drew the polo over his head and handed it to me. My eyes locked on his stomach, on the ripples his abs created. Clearing my throat, I looked up—not at him, but past him and snatched the shirt from his grasp. No wonder he was smug, he had the stomach of an MMA fighter.

I ran to the back and grabbed the rubbing alcohol, I dabbed on Royce's shirt—having done this to my own clothes a couple dozen times. I knew to be patient and to dab, no rubbing. Within five minutes I had the stain out. I hurried to the front, and there stood Royce, one arm over the bar of my mixer looking into Neal's white and pink spiraled cake—shirtless.

It was like a scene from a baker's dream calendar. Thankful no customers had come into the shop, I tossed Royce his shirt, damp in two spots, but stain-free.

"Um, you need to put that on."

"Yes, ma'am." He slipped back into his shirt, then picked up Neal's card once more.

I turned in toward the counter, hiding what felt like an obnoxious, epic blush, then turned the mixer onto low. The whisk spun in a slow figure eight. I heard as he tore open the sealed envelope behind me and withdrew the card.

I scratched my neck and peeked at him, but when I couldn't see his full expression, I turned around. His brows scrunched together and his eyes studied the word on the card. He looked all together confused or maybe surprised, I couldn't tell. How shocking could it be—boy or girl, those were the only options, right?

"What?" I stretched my neck, maybe I could see what it said. "I'm right, aren't I?" I swallowed, I wasn't supposed to care. That was the point. This was just another reveal. Right or wrong—I didn't care!

"Well…" he said, drawing out the word, but not answering my question.

I threw my head back, darting a glance at the ceiling. "What? Just show me."

"I'm not sure you want to—"

I snatched the card from his hands. Looking down at the white card, my eyes ran over the black script. "Huh."

"So," he said, "you aren't right."

"But I'm not wrong either." I dropped the card onto the counter. "Twins."

"One boy," he said, "one girl."

A delirious laugh bubbled from my throat and out of my mouth. Pink or blue—neither would mess up his gender reveal. Not completely, anyway.

I shrugged. "It's a stupid cake. It doesn't matter."

"Blake," Royce said, setting a hand to my shoulder, "please don't call anything you bake stupid. I'd give my right eye for a slice of your cake."

I full-on rolled my eyes and sputtered a raspberry from my lips. "You are a dork." But my heart thumped with his words. He really loved my cake.

He lifted his brows. "It's not a lie. It's that good." He cleared his throat and crossed his arms over his chest. "But here's what I'm thinking. We are mature adults. This is *important*. We cannot mess with Neal and Patricia's big day. We have to be honest."

My lip curled with his words.

Then, Royce picked up the blue bottle of dye and scooping out a heap double the size I would have used, he slopped it into the mixing bowl—the one already filled with pink batter—and turned on the spin cycle.

The blue mixed into the fuchsia batter, turning it into a deep purple. "There," he said, smacking his hands together, "perfect."

I snickered, one hand on my hip. "Yes. Perfect." I pulled the three readied cake pans from the shelf beneath the counter and dumped part of the dark purple cake inside each.

An hour and a half later, Neal's cakes had baked and cooled. I sat in front of them—Royce still in my shop, watching me work.

"So, you don't have to go to work today?" I asked. We'd discussed his ideas for the festival cake. They weren't bad—I'd use them, actually. He wanted me to create cherry blossom flowers to swirl along the outside. I could do that—it would be a challenge, but I liked a challenge.

He ignored my question and watched as I dumped Neal's purple cakes from their pans. "Why so many cakes?"

"Watch. I'll layer them with icing in the middle. Normally the icing would be part of the reveal, but in this case, I'm going to keep it white."

I dipped into my prepared butter icing and slathered it onto the first cake. I topped it with the second cake and followed the same procedure.

"You're so quick. Can I try?"

"Um, *no.*" I shook my head. This wasn't cooking class. This was my job. Sure, I messed with the gender reveal, but the look and taste of the cake kept me employed.

"Come on," he whined. "It's *Neal's* cake."

"Meh." I paused my work, shrugged one shoulder, and handed him the icing knife.

He spread, back and forth, struggling to smooth out the top. He tried again, this time moving the knife into the cake and creating a small crack in the purple mass. "Oh—" he hissed, scrunching his nose. "Sorry."

"Move. I'll cover it with frosting." I held out my hand, like a surgeon asking for their next scalpel. I fixed his small blunder and began on the sides, spinning my cake board as I quickly wrapped the frosting around the three-layered cake.

I glanced at Royce who watched my cake like one of those calming YouTube videos—unable to take his eyes off. Once I'd slathered on a thin white layer of my butter icing, I dyed a small portion pink and another blue. Then I wrapped the bottom in blue, left a small middle of white, and then went over the top third in pink. I melted white chocolate and dripped it around and down the sides of the cake, giving it a paint-dripping effect. Then I spun on a white border and called it good.

"I—" He tilted his head, looking at my cake in between long blinks. "Wow. That was impressive."

I gave a quick chortle. "That was quick and simple. Just a result of a lot of practice."

He looked at me with scrutiny in his eyes. "I don't think you know how good you are."

My cheeks warmed again and I turned away, gathering my bowls and taking them into the back kitchen.

Royce followed me through, though. I ignored him, thinking Christian would scare him off, but my boss must have been in his office because he was nowhere to be found in the main kitchen.

"So," Royce said, "what time does he pick up the cake?"

I glanced up at the clock on the wall. "Oh, shoot. Ten minutes."

"I'll give it to him."

"Don't you have your own job to be at?" I started filling the sink basin with suds, then dried my hands, hurrying back out front to box the cake.

His brows rose. "I do actually. My assistant is taking care of a few things today. I wanted to help... take care of..."

Darting my eyes his way, I glared—he best not say that he wanted to take care of *me*.

He breathed out. "Um—the *Cherry Festival*." He stood tall, sliding one hand into his pocket. Dipping his head, his eyes met mine. "Blake, I don't mind giving it to him. You don't have to see him."

Ugh. His offer only brought back the memory of me *crying*… in the kitchen… on the ground… right in front of him—practically a stranger.

"Royce, I realize because of my spectacle last week you might see me as a soft, scared little girl—" I shut my eyes and bobbed my head to my chest once before glaring at him again. "However," I said, straightening my shoulders, believing my next words, "I am an independent, strong woman. We can't always be damsels in distress."

He peered down at me, at least half a foot taller than my measly 5'6. "I didn't call you a damsel in distress, Blake. I just thought I'd take something uncomfortable off your plate."

"Thanks," I said—my tone not all that thankful. "But if you did that, then I wouldn't have the chance to make Neal feel uncomfortable."

Despite my not-so-friendly tone, the right side of his lips quirked up in a smile. Okay, so I didn't *not* like Royce Valentine. Still, I wouldn't be telling Juliana that.

Then for some dumb reason—that smile and me not hating Royce, softened my tone. "As well as scare him a little," I said, talking about Neal. I bounced my brows. "Believe me, he will be terrified to eat this cake when he finds out that I'm the one who made it."

CHAPTER SEVENTEEN

Jack

*W*arm air blew in through the vent of the men's bathroom, making me muggy and much too warm. "What do you think?"

"I think this is stupid."

I set down my bottle of cologne and turned to meet Royce head-on. Eye to eye. He could state his opinion. I wouldn't cower. "Did you want to be more specific?"

"You're asking her to meet you in an hour."

"So?" I turned back to the mirror.

"So, what if she's busy? What if she has a work meeting?"

"That's kind of the point."

"Dude," Royce ran a hand through his hair as if he were truly invested in my non-existent relationship with Juliana. "So, your point is—choose, me or your job? Cause we both know, at this stage in the game, you're gonna lose that battle. Besides, what does that say about you?"

I knit my brows. I'd been so confident in this plan. "Surely, she has a lunch hour. It isn't an ultimatum lunch."

Roy rolled his eyes. "Have you met this girl? *Surely,* she works through lunch."

I scoffed—though he had a point. "You don't know Juliana."

"No, but she's all you talk about and I do know Blake pretty well by now."

I pulled my head back in offense. "Juliana is nothing like Blake."

But Royce shook his head. "Then you don't know her sister. They are both passionate about work. They don't shy away from a challenge and they're willing to take risks."

I stared at my cousin. Was he defending Blake? Then, I turned back to the mirror, throwing a comb through my hair. "If I didn't know better, I'd think you might be starting to like Blake."

"I don't like her." He shrugged—in a very non-Royce way. "I just don't despise her anymore."

"Huh." I turned back to him, feeling a little better in my appearance. "That sounds like the same thing."

He ignored my comment and followed me out of the bathroom. "At least Blake was willing to take a chance on love. It's not her fault she was burned."

"Maybe it was. Do you know what happened?" I don't know why I disagreed with him. Arguing with Royce never worked out in my favor. Besides, I liked giving people the benefit of the doubt —normally. Still, Blake? We'd both seen her at Mom's dinner party. She wasn't exactly sunshine and roses.

"Yes," he said, but his pitch rang too high for confidence. He didn't know the whole story. I couldn't believe he defended her.

"Well, is she taking a chance again? Because I thought you planned to get her out of her slump by going on a few dates and then letting her dump you."

He scratched the back of his neck, then moved over to his 5 o'clock shadow—thinking. "I'm working on it. I just need time."

"Well, I'm actually going to ask my girl out. Good luck with time," I said walking over to my desk.

"When did you get so cocky, little cousin." He leaned his backside against my desk, arms crossed, scrutinizing me.

"Cocky?" I glanced back at him. "Believe me when I tell you I am not." In fact, I could use some of your confidence. "I'm pretty sure this plan is going to fail miserably. But I'd rather try and fail ninety-nine nights in a row if it meant I got to spend one evening with Juliana."

He looked at me as if his gag reflex was about to kick in. "Let me know how it goes." He stood up to go. "What night are you on anyway? Is this fifty-six? Eighty-two? How many more do you have to suffer through before she shows up?" He raised his brows and left me.

I ignored him, enticed by the thought of an hour with Juliana. Royce would not detour me. I pulled out my phone and texted:

Lunch is in one hour. I'll be at Benny's Bar & Grill. Meet me?

I stared at my phone, waiting for Juliana's conversation bubbles to pop up. When they didn't, I looked at my desk. One file lay out of place, everything else sat prim and neat, right where it should be. I picked up the file and flipped through my notes on the Elderberry site. It was mostly up and working… just a few adjustments that needed attending.

Warmed by the air still blowing through the vents of the office building, I tugged on my collar. Then, I peeked at my phone again. Nothing.

Tapping my foot, I opened my laptop. I had an hour until lunch —I'd get these bugs out of the website I'd been working on. It would take five minutes, maybe ten.

A note flashed on my computer screen—"Updates," I read

aloud, mumbling to myself, "restart your computer." Without a second thought, I clicked *ok*—forgetting all the bugs I'd planned to fix, and set my computer into restart mode.

Snatching my phone from the desk, I typed in *Benny's* to my maps. "Eleven minutes." Then I typed in Juliana's work and *Benny's*. "Four minutes." I tapped my toe. I could leave a little early. Mom wouldn't care. Especially if I actually got to see Juliana.

Distracted by the map lines on my phone, I jumped when my computer sang, announcing it had returned to life. I set my phone to the side but switched it back to my messages—with no new notifications. I pulled up the Elderberry site and glanced at my phone—I could have sworn it lit up.

Maybe she wouldn't reply. Maybe she didn't want to see me. After all, I had called her selfish not that long ago. I'd meant it well —loving even. I could see every possible beauty in Juliana. Selfishness in any form would never fit her personality. Sure, she worked too hard. But juggling life is difficult. Maybe I'd made a mistake in mentioning it. Maybe I should have kept my opinion to myself. As much as I wanted her to like me though, I couldn't hide the real me. Straightforwardness and all.

Running through numbers and codes, I fixed the two malfunctioning buttons on the site I'd built for Elderberry Pharmaceuticals. I sent them a quick email, letting them know the kinks had been worked out, then checked the time on the screen. Thirty-two minutes until lunch, minus eleven for the drive. Then I peered down at my watch—but it gave me the exact same information.

My phone lit up next to me. I scooped up the device and swiped to unlock the screen. My shoulders slumped when I saw Royce's name at the top of my messages.

Where are you going for lunch?

I typed a quick response.

```
Nice try.
```

Like I'd give him that. I didn't need Royce's help. He wasn't going to show up to *Benny's* and try to Roxanne this situation.

Still, I laughed when he said,

```
I'm not going to Roxanne you. I'm just hungry
                and need ideas.
```

Our grandma had made us watch that old Steve Martin film. Neither of us cared for the chick-flick, filmed long before our births. Except now, as I thought about it, Steve does get the girl in the end—big nose and all. *Mistakes* and all.

But Royce—no, Royce would not be helping me get any girl. I just needed to be myself. To have confidence.

Aw crap. I sounded exactly like Mom. I didn't want Mom or Royce on our date.

Then again—was it a date? I hadn't said, *can I take you on a date*. I darted a glance to my phone screen. And apparently, Juliana wasn't going to respond at all.

So... yeah, probably couldn't count it as a date.

With fourteen minutes until lunch and no response from Juliana, I left for *Benny's Bar & Grill.* Maybe she wouldn't respond, but what if she still came?

I couldn't take that chance. I couldn't be absent if she came.

Royce watched me from his standing desk in our open office area. With my departure, he gave me a big thumbs up. I swallowed, trying not to look at him.

Breathing in the tropical sweetness of my car air freshener, I sat in *Benny's* parking lot for two minutes.

Still no reply from Juliana.

I could leave. I could turn around and go and pretend the whole thing didn't happen. *I didn't make a fool of myself and Juliana never rejected me.*

But then...

What if she did come?

If she came, and I wasn't here—after I said I would be—that would be so much worse than my pride taking a hit.

I stepped from the car and started inside. I had to eat, right?

"How many, sir?" the hostess asked.

"Um—one." I bobbed my head from side to side. "Possibly two, but possibly not."

She smiled, but somehow it greatly resembled a frown. "So..." she held up her menu.

"Um, just—just one menu. I'll share with her if she's able to make it." I followed the girl through the restaurant and to the table, my nervous tongue rambling. "She's busy. It's pretty much a fifty-fifty chance if she'll have time to leave work. You just never know. She's dedicated. Work takes time." And just like that—I started quoting Kelly Clarkson songs.

I needed to do fifty pushups and get out all this nervous energy. I never skipped the gym, but I should have done a double session today.

I sat, tapping my toe on the tiled floor of the restaurant and the frown-smiling girl handed me my one and only menu. I bowed my head, looking down at the thing, then looked up to the empty seat across from me.

Royce was right. I was an idiot.

"She isn't coming," I said aloud. "It's fine."

An older woman sitting at the table to the left of me reached out her hand and patted my shoulder—listening to my one-sided conversation. "You're very handsome," she said.

"What?" My eyes bulged as I stared at the graying curly haired woman.

I didn't need Royce, my mother, or any elderly eavesdroppers at my lunch.

Twenty minutes later—

"Jack, she's only twelve minutes late. Have faith, son, she'll

97

come." Scotty, my new eavesdropping elderly friend's husband, had turned his chair so that it faced my table.

Linda—the eavesdropper, Scotty's wife, reached for my hand. "Juliana would be foolish to leave you here by yourself. She isn't dating anyone and you're such a catch," Linda said, while Scotty nodded with his wife's declaration. "Here you are, waiting here for her. She is lucky to have someone as patient and good-looking as you in her life."

I tried to smile, but it only made me picture the smiling-frown of the hostess earlier.

"Well, sure she is. There isn't a better man. You've got a steady job, a great family," Scotty said.

Linda pointed at him, "Don't forget, he volunteers at the humane society every Sunday."

"That's right. You're the entire package, my boy. If our son can settle down—you'll have no problem."

I nodded at Scotty, who had more hair than any eighty-year-old man I'd ever met. "Thanks. I mean, Lee is the manager at Costco now. He's accomplished a lot in ten years."

Linda grinned at the mention of their eldest son's name.

In twenty-five minutes, I'd learned about Scotty and Linda's two sons, their cat Fatso, and Scotty's recent retirement; and they had learned about me. They spoke to me as if they'd known me my entire life.

Twenty-eight minutes into our lunch hour, Linda and Scotty had their chairs scooted right up to my table, Linda's iced tea even rested on my tabletop, when—Juliana walked through the door.

I gulped, staring at the entrance. "Hey," I hissed under my breath, "she's here!"

Both Scotty and Linda whipped their heads to the entrance.

Linda's sweet wrinkled smile went flat. Her gaze turned toward me and her eyes dimmed. "That's her?"

I nodded, small shakes of my head. Waving one hand, I silently shooed them back to their own table.

"Whew." Scotty blew out a breath. Then he grunted. "Good luck, Jack."

Linda looked at me—all at once, no longer impressed. "You're gonna need it."

CHAPTER EIGHTEEN

Juliana

"You made it!" Jack stood to greet me as an elderly couple scooched their chairs from his table over to the table at his left, their eyes on me.

I knit my brows. "Did—did you have friends join you?"

"Um, yeah for a minute. They have their own table." Jack didn't bother to introduce us and the giant grin the older woman gave me made me a tad grateful I didn't have to make small talk.

I sat across from him and crossed my legs, my right knee hitting the top of the table. "Sorry, I'm late. I… well, work was crazy. Then, I sat for two seconds to scarf down a veggie wrap and saw your text."

He nodded. "No—no worries. I mean, I'm just glad it worked out."

"Yeah, well, I left a load on my desk, but I figured you were here and you must have news." I breathed out—full from the wrap that I stuffed down too quickly.

"Oh—news? Um, I mean, everything's coming along with Mom and Charlotte—you probably know better than I do."

I gave a short laugh. "No—with Blake. That's why you asked me here, right?"

"Oh. *Blake*," he said and he seemed more jittery than normal. "Well, not really. Things are progressing. She's got the job."

My brows knit together. "So..." What had he asked me here for?

"I just—"

"Hey!" The waitress stood at our table. "Your friend finally showed up." The girl, with the tag reading Wendy, gave Jack a big thumbs up, her lips parting into a giant grin. "Nice!"

He returned the grin, but it seemed forced. "Yeah. Uh, do you want a drink? Did you need a minute to see a menu?"

Wendy held a paper menu out to me, as if on cue.

I shook my head, feeling irritated wrinkles spread across my forehead. "No. I already ate."

Wendy didn't lose her excitement, "Water? Soda? We have Pepsi products."

I shut my eyes, willing the girl to go away. "Water." I opened them and ignored the girl writing down my simple beverage order. I stared at Jack. "Then what? Jack, I took on a new job this week. Between your sister's wedding, Andrea Leawood's Oscar dress, and now Amy Allen's photoshoot—I am totally swamped. Not to mention all of Mark's jobs that I have to wrap up." I rubbed a finger over my forehead—not allowing the memory of Jack Anderson calling me selfish to enter my mind. Surely, he thought me even more selfish with my happy news of country singer Amy Allen hiring me. Maybe that's why my defenses rose so quickly.

"I thought lunch might be nice. We both have to eat."

"I ate while I worked." I couldn't keep the disdain from my voice.

His eyes turned to slits. "You took a new job? I thought you were booked until the end of the year."

I sighed, unsure why I hadn't left yet. "I am. But Amy Allen asked for me, Jack." I still couldn't believe it. She was all anyone talked about in the country music industry right now. "Her family is part of a People magazine photoshoot—and she wants me to be their designer."

"But you're booked."

"Yes. But it's *Amy Allen*. It's *People* magazine. You'd do the same. If *People* magazine asked you to create a website for them, you'd add it to your already overloaded to-do list."

But Jack just looked at me—and not like he normally looked at me—soft and sweet, but confused and almost irritated himself. What reason did he have to be annoyed with me? "No," he said, "I wouldn't."

He judged me. *Again*. I could see it all over his face. I thought he said he liked me. But here he sat judging me. He'd called me selfish. "Then, you won't be very successful," I said.

"I guess that depends on your definition of success."

I scoffed. "And what's your definition, Jack?"

"Happiness, I guess. Doing something I love. But more so being with those I love."

His definition made my skin prickle a little.

And then he added, "It isn't based on how high I rise."

For some dumb reason, tears sprung to my eyes. I held them back, more frustrated than ever with Jack Anderson. "Why did you ask me here, Jack?"

"I told you, Juliana, I like you. I was hoping to spend some time with you."

I sniffed and blinked one long blink, making sure my tears stayed in my head. "How can you like me? You don't know me. Not really."

"Do you really believe that?" he said with a sad smile. "You've been working with my family for a year."

"That's work."

"Which apparently," he said, motioning a hand, palm flat, out toward me, "is life."

I pursed my lips, biting back the jumbled angry nonsense in my head.

"Besides, I do know you, Jewels," he said, using Blake's nickname for me. "You're smart—like brilliant. You have a shy sense of humor, but I've seen it," he grinned, his eyes sliding from the wooden table we sat at to my face, "and it's pretty fantastic. You work hard—but that's obvious. Still, I don't know that anyone pays attention to details the way that you do. You take handwritten notes, but add sticky notes to them later with thoughts and ideas that come to you at other times. You research your clients long before you meet them."

I eyed him—how did he know that?

"You called me Jack the first time we met—not Jackson, not *Mr. Kucho*. No one introduced us, you just *knew*. You also wore that blue dress—the one with the little collar," he motioned at his neck, his lips turning up slightly. "That shade is now Charlotte's main wedding color. And I'm not sure how you knew she'd love it—but you did. I could tell.

"You're also loving and tender." His blue-green eyes found my lips for the briefest of seconds, before returning my gaze. "You love your sister fiercely, though you don't know how to help her—or how to take enough time for her."

"Hey—" I began, but he kept going.

"Your father is important to you. But you don't see him that often—not as often as you'd like to, anyway. He raised you alone, for the most part. But I'm not sure what happened to your mother."

My eyes filled again with his words. How had he watched me so closely to figure all this out? What did I do in my everyday life to tell him all this?

"You're dedicated—*so* dedicated." He grinned again. "But you're also getting stretched pretty thin, Juliana. It's hard to spread that dedication out. Something will always lose."

I grit my teeth with the truth. I was spread thin, as much as I wanted to deny it. I couldn't.

"You're also *the* most gorgeous woman I've ever met." He cleared his throat. "But you don't know it. It isn't fake or an act. You just really have no idea how naturally lovely you are."

A lump formed in my throat and I blinked six too many times.

That's when I noticed the waitress, standing there, holding my water, with tears on her cheeks.

Jack's friends at the table next to ours, stared, the woman with her hands clasped at her heart and the man beaming at Jack like a proud papa.

I licked my lips. "I—I should go," I said, my tone hushed. I purposely did not look at the people around us—the eyes watching us. I stood, almost tipping my chair over backward, and clicked my heels toward the exit.

"Jewels," he called. "Juliana! Wait." The patter of his shoes tapped behind me, but I hurried out the doors and into the parking lot.

My pencil skirt made it difficult to rush, but I careened my way out to my Mazda—the sun shining off its silver coat—in sixty seconds.

"Juliana," he said behind me.

Through my peripheral, I could see him reach out, and I turned to face him.

"I'm—I'm sorry. I didn't mean to upset you."

"Or *judge* me?" I swallowed. I preferred throwing the judgment back at him than addressing everything else he'd said or how it had made me feel.

His brows knit. "No—I mean," he crammed his eyes shut, "I guess I did that. But only because I like you. I want you to be happy."

I blinked in the sunshine, looking straight across, into his hazel eyes. At five foot ten and in four-inch heels, I could just about meet him eye to eye. "How did you know about my father?"

"You mentioned him once."

I furrowed my brows, thinking. Had I? I didn't remember.

"Charlotte talked about our dad one day. It was just for a minute, but then you mentioned how your dad used to brush your hair at night when you were little."

"I did?" I whispered the words—they were for myself, not Jack. I didn't remember, but that had always been a tender memory for me—Daddy brushing my hair at night before I'd go to bed. He always tried to make sure I wouldn't have tangles in the morning. "But you knew he raised us alone."

"I deducted."

I stared at him, almost disbelieving.

"I'm observant."

I looked at Jack, trying to see him the way he saw me. He was handsome and smart. He was kind and well-off—his family had money—that was no secret. But what else did I know? I knew his mother, his sister, his father a little—but I didn't know how he felt about any of them. How did he see so much? And what had I missed? "What do you see now?" I asked.

He wet his lips, his eyes roving over my face, from my hair to my chin. "I see a girl trying to do it all. I see someone who needs to give themselves a little grace."

I lifted one brow, unsure of what he meant.

"Time. You need time for yourself, Juliana. You need time for your family. Work and passion are wonderful, but they won't ever replace the people who care about you." He scratched at the nape of his neck. "And sure, it sounds really convenient for me to say all that when I'm asking to be one of those people. When I'd like some of that precious time. But I'd like to be someone you allow to care for you. Truly though, if you never spend another minute with me —you still need time, for you." He lifted his hand, circling his finger in my direction as he spoke. "For *you.*"

And—I believed him.

That's when I decided I liked Jack Anderson—more than just a little. I leaned in, blinking back the moisture in my eyes, and breathed him in—peppermint and earth. I set my lips to his soft, shaven cheek, lingering there a few seconds longer than I should have. I pulled back, taking a second to study his eyes—those blue-green, sea-like, hazel eyes. They were honest eyes. He said he wanted me to be happy and I believed him.

"I'll see you, Jack," I said just above a whisper, my breath tickling his cheek. Then I slid into the cab of my car and drove back to work.

CHAPTER NINETEEN

Royce

I would not let Blake Minola destroy my ego.

Sure, I may have asked her out a couple times. She may have rejected me. Every. Single. Time. But that was more about her—not me.

The trouble is—I thought we'd connected at the bakery. I mean, I'd enjoyed our day together rather than feeling like I fulfilled a duty to win a promotion. It seemed like she'd enjoyed it too. But that didn't stop her from rejecting my dinner invite.

The next day, I mindlessly scrolled through my phone, sitting at the table just outside Blake's bakery. The windows allowed me to see inside and I wore my dark sunglasses while watching her as she worked at the front kitchen counter.

I hadn't noticed before how graceful she moved. She'd always appeared to be moving in for the kill, but when she baked she appeared to be a well-choreographed dancer. She smiled as she worked too. I didn't know what she worked on, but it wasn't a gender reveal. Those only made her growl and cringe. Today she smiled. She may have *glowed*.

I pulled down my glasses—maybe my head imagined her glow. Maybe the hue from my lenses had created the radiance.

Busy watching Blake's glow—I missed the couple entering the building. But as if someone had flipped a switch—the blaze in her face dissipated into dying, angry embers.

Blake slapped on her false interested face, listened to the couple, jotted down a note, then took the card from the pregnant woman's hands. As the couple turned to leave, she seemed to gag for the briefest of seconds.

I laughed, watching her clearly disgusted face.

I wanted to know what she'd been making before. I wanted to know why it made her face light up in that pretty way.

She flung her dark ponytail from her shoulder and went back to work. I watched, waiting for any clues. None came, and then suddenly she removed her apron and brushed her slender hands on the thighs of her tight jeans. She walked around the counter and pulled the rubber band from her hair, shaking out the ponytail. Then she started for the front entrance.

"Crap." I shot from my seat at the small patio table outside *Much Ado About Cakes*. I took a step left—then right, then hid behind a light pole, leaning against the thing and pretending to look out at the street.

I heard as the door opened and closed, then peeked backward when Blake's footsteps seemed to grow quieter. The sign on the shop door now read—closed for lunch.

"Huh." She hadn't closed for lunch the day I'd been there.

Turning on my heels, I began to follow her, just ten steps behind. I hadn't planned on becoming a stalker today—it just sort of happened.

Geoni's Deli sat at the end of the block and she walked as if on a mission—I followed, sure we'd end our trek there. But she crossed the street away from Geoni's and straight toward an old bookstore.

I'd been inside the place once before, it looked small from the outside, but seemed to go on forever once inside. I waited a minute, then followed Blake inside the building. She stood at the counter near the front, so I ducked behind a bookcase, pretending to pull something off the shelf. With my eyes hidden behind my sunglasses, I spied her.

She grinned at the old man behind the counter. I moved a little closer—hoping to hear her better.

"That's okay," she said, waving off whatever the older man had just said to her. "It's Blake. Blake Minola."

Flipping through an old, wooden, catalog box, he searched through cataloged cards. Not exactly an efficient system for today's age, but it seemed to work for him. He pulled one out, holding it up for Blake to see. "Yes, but see here," he held the card out to her. "I could only find it used."

Blake shrugged, not from boredom, but as if new or used didn't matter. "That's great," she said, and she spoke to him in a way I'd never heard her talk to anyone—respectfully. "That will only give it more character. He'll love it."

He? Who—who was *he*? Had Blake turned me down three times because she was already seeing someone? I didn't like the way that made my gut turn. I shouldn't care—but I did.

Blake Minola had more to her than I thought possible. Maybe I could only admit it to myself, but I found myself captivated when figuring her out.

I pulled my baseball cap down farther and studied Blake as she waited for whatever the old shop owner disappeared to find. She didn't scroll on her phone or look through the aisles of books. She tapped her toe, chewed on her thumbnail, and peered at her wrist-watch—twice.

It only took the man four minutes to return. He carried a book, no bigger than a piece of 8x10 printer paper with a blank front and a tattered blue cover. The binding said something in gold embossed letters, but I was too far away to read it.

Blake turned, so I could see just the side of her face, her mouth turned up in the most joyful grin.

"Who is this guy?" I said, just loud enough for me to hear—and apparently, the lady standing right next to me. I snatched a book from the shelf—hoping to appear as a shopper and not a prowler. I opened the book but watched Blake and the shopkeeper through my dark lenses.

"When is the trip?" the shopkeeper asked, he studied Blake as she carefully turned page after page of the old book.

"The end of May."

"Just a few weeks then."

"Yes. Your timing is perfect." She held the book to her chest.

She was going on a trip... with some guy? But I couldn't land a simple dinner date?

"This is crap," I said. I'd forgotten about the woman next to me until she inched one step closer and eyed the book in my hands. She lifted one brow, her eyes drawing from the book to my face.

Blake must have paid because she started for the exit. I slid my book back onto the shelf, seeing its title on the binding for the first time. *17 Ways to Please Your Lover.*

"I don't need that," I said to the older woman, who didn't hide her interest in my reading material. "Excuse me," I said, working my way past the lady.

Blake scampered back across the street, to Gioni's, her prized book in a bag. She didn't hold it by the handle, but wrapped one arm protectively around the thing, keeping it at her chest. My heart thumped with annoyance.

I waited, watching through the window until she had her order —she sat at one of the empty tables and pulled her book from the bag. Nibbling on her deli sandwich, she carefully turned each page.

I pushed open the entrance, aggravation fueling my actions. I walked right past her and placed my own order with the kid at the counter. "Turkey and bacon on rye. No mayo, no pickles. Can I get a bag of chips?"

The kid quietly produced my order, but I kept talking, making sure my voice was heard above the hum of discussion in the room.

"Do you have bottled water?"

A nod from my sandwich maker.

"Two of those. And one of those chocolate chip cookies."

I glanced over my shoulder. Blake's back faced the lunch counter, but her head had lifted, she turned her face to the side, listening.

I paid the clerk and snatched my sack of food. I walked her way —purposely not looking in her direction. She ate cake with me, while turning me down for dinner, and bought books for some other guy. I would walk past her. I wouldn't speak.

"Royce?" she said and her tone held a question, but not the disdain I'd become used to. She talked to me like she spoke to that bookstore owner—with a little delight in her voice. Which only annoyed me more—that delight came from this book, this other guy.

Not me.

"Oh, hey." I stopped, but tried to act as if her presence didn't affect me.

"What are you doing here?"

I held up my bag—irritated that I secretly wished she'd invite me to sit. "Lunch."

"Oh," she shook her head, "right. Is your work close to 16th Street?"

"Uh—not really. But I like Gioni's."

She nodded.

"What are *you* doing here?" I said, too much accusation in my voice. "I've never seen you take a lunch break before?"

Her brows waxed—one above the other and her gaze became piercing. "You've only spent two days in the shop with me. Maybe I didn't take a lunch because of you."

111

I laughed—liking the way the angst crept into her voice. Then, as if her cranky tone were an invitation, I sat across from her. "What are you reading?" I said, my eyes darting to the old book with the tattered blue cover and yellowed pages. I spotted a map on the left page and writing on the right—but my glance didn't last long enough for any of it to make any sense.

"Oh," she said, shutting the book. "I wasn't—not really."

"Is it a classic? It looks old." I pressed—I wanted to know. And I wanted to know who she planned to share it with.

She shook her head, her brunette hair swaying at her shoulders. "No." She cleared her throat. "It's just a guidebook."

"A guidebook? Where are you going?" My head argued with itself—*sure, that sounded natural... No, no it did not.*

"Um, *nowhere*." Her eyes widened, as if she wished she were going somewhere... or maybe as if she'd slug me if I kept prying.

But wasn't she planning a trip? I'd heard the shop owner ask about her travels. I'd heard her answer—*May*. Why would she lie to me?

"Then, what's with the book? I don't follow."

She blew out a puff of air. "My dad is taking a trip. It's the first time he's gone anywhere by himself. It's his birthday and I bought him this old guidebook. Okay?"

"Huh," I hummed, genuinely surprised. Her *dad*—not some guy, but her dad. With my bizarre, foreign jealousy at bay, I looked more closely at her book, her gift to her dad. "Why not get him a new one?"

She bit her full bottom lip and I wondered what that lip might taste like. Clearing my throat, I forced my gaze up to her honey, golden eyes. "My great grandparents grew up in Scotland. My dad wants to visit their old homes and land. This was the only book I could find with maps of those places." She lifted one shoulder. "It's out of date, but he'll like it. Hopefully, it'll have some use." Her brows knit. "And hopefully he'll still use GPS and this baby won't get him totally lost."

I studied her. She had spoken—had told me something *personal* —and she hadn't growled once. I blinked, bringing myself back to the present. "That's really nice, Blake."

Tugging on the ends of her hair, she pressed her lips together. "Yeah, well, sometimes I can be nice."

That made me laugh—which made her smile.

I pulled my lunch from its sack, waiting for her to protest, when she didn't, I took a bite of my turkey on rye. "Can I take a look?"

"Uh—sure. Wipe off your hands." She held a napkin out to me.

I chuckled under my breath. "No problem." I took the white restaurant napkin, my fingers brushing hers, just a bit, a touch so small I'm surprised I even noticed it. Then I wiped my already clean hands on the napkin. She watched, then slid her book in front of me. I skimmed through a few pages. "This is cool. So, you're Scottish eh?"

"I guess. Mostly, I'm Coloradoan." She took a bite of her sandwich.

"What are you eating?" I asked, tilting my head to see her order better.

"Salami, pepperoni, and banana peppers."

I scrunched my face in disgust.

"Don't knock it, till you've tried it."

"Are you offering me a bite?"

She scoffed. "No."

"Fine, let's meet back here for dinner. I'll order one myself."

She eyed me, warily. "I can't."

"You mean, you won't." I kept my eyes on hers—unafraid and challenging her to look away first.

"*I mean,* I have plans. It's my dad's birthday. So, unless you want to eat with a father, and his two daughters, and talk about the weather in Scotland in May, it's a no-go."

I couldn't stop my grin. I squared my shoulders and said, "I'd love to."

"You'd love to what?"

I pointed at her, then picked up my turkey on rye. "You just invited me to dinner with you and your dad. I'd love to go. Thanks, Blake."

"I—no—I..." Her glance darted from one end of the room to the other. She couldn't dispute that she'd invited me—accident or not.

Which meant, I finally had a date with Blake.

CHAPTER TWENTY

Blake

Juliana tugged on my shirt, pulling me toward her until I almost sat on top of her. "I can't believe you invited a guy to Dad's dinner," she hissed in my ear.

Dad's thirty-year-old couch had impressions that had impressions—once you were in it, getting out was a challenge. That might have been the only thing keeping me in place with her tug. "So what?" I said, sending a sharp elbow into her side—just like I used to when we'd argue at twelve and eleven.

"Ouch!" she yelped. "*Blake,*" her eyes went wide with her glare.

"Sorry—it's instinct. This house turns me back into a twelve-year-old."

"It really does." Her frown deepened as she looked me over. "I have no idea why you'd want to bring someone home with the way you behave!"

"Shh!" I resisted elbowing her again as the bathroom door opened and Royce came striding out.

It was weird... Royce was here... in my childhood home, and

sure, I hadn't meant to invite him, but I still couldn't believe he'd even come. No way I'd tell Jewels about my accidental invitation. She could go on thinking I'd meant to include him.

"Blake-berry, that cake looks outstanding." Dad walked into the room, his short strides and slight limp had my head in Scotland. How would he get around? What if he needed help? Could he do this alone?

Royce's mouth turned up in a mischievous grin. He mouthed to me—"*Blakeberry?*"

I rolled my eyes at him, my lips twitching with the desire to smile, while my legs itched to run away.

"Dinner's almost ready. I just need to sauce the burgers."

Oh, burger-gravy—Dad's favorite meal.

Juliana stood and strode over to our father, setting a hand on his back. He only stood a couple inches taller than her now, he'd shrunk over the years. "I wished you'd let me cook. It's your birthday."

"Oh no, dear." He held a hand to my sister's face. "My gift is having both of my girls home and at my table. And having Roy here." He motioned a hand toward Royce.

"It's Royce, Dad." I stood too, running my sweaty palms down the sides of my thighs.

"That's okay, *Blakeberry*. Plenty of my friends call me Roy."

Dad smiled at him, he seemed to like Royce. But then he liked Neal, too. Not that I should be comparing the two. Royce was a client who, at times, felt like a friend. Sort of.

"Come on, Roy," Dad said. "Do you cook? You can help me in the kitchen."

I bit my lip. *Oh, crap.*

"I'm twenty-nine and single, William. I better be able to cook or I might starve."

Dad chuckled. "Twenty-nine? I've got you beat. Sixty-eight, single, and Parkinson's. And it's just Will."

Juliana and I shared a look, then followed after the pair into the kitchen.

Dad's burgers sizzled on the stovetop. He had rice in the rice cooker and a gravy packet waiting for him. Yep, he loved this meal. And though it may not have been very fancy or even traditional, as kids, Juliana and I loved it too.

"You start the gravy," Dad said, pointing a finger to the packet on the counter. I swore, with his mention of the word: *Parkinson's*, his finger suddenly tremored.

I swallowed, watching him. He hadn't progressed much— besides his shuffling feet. He said his legs just didn't feel strong anymore.

"I can do that, Dad." I hurried to the counter, to where Royce stood, and snatched up the gravy mix.

"I've got it," Royce said, peering down at me. He felt too close in the quaint kitchen and with my family standing there. I could smell the mint on his breath and my head had me feeling the thump of his beating heart, just inches from mine—or maybe that was just my heart beating spastically.

He held out his hand for the gravy mix.

"Let Roy do it, Blakeberry. You made the cake." Dad took the mix from my hands and laid it in Royce's palm. "Doesn't that cake look good, Roy?" Dad's eyes darted to the cake I'd made earlier that day.

"It does. I mean, it's green… with real flowers on it, but it looks… amazing."

Juliana laughed, then covered her mouth with her hand.

"It's a matcha pistachio cake. And you don't eat the flowers." I crossed my arms, defending my masterpiece.

"It's Dad's favorite," Juliana explained.

"Because it's her best," Dad said. "Wait until you try it, Roy. You'll never want another cake again."

"I believe it," Royce peered at me, though he spoke to Dad. "I've already decided that, from now on, I won't eat cake unless Blake is the one to bake it. Anything else would just disappoint me."

My heart seemed to patter quicker—over cake talk. His dark eyes bore into me until I had to look away. I might break if I didn't.

I walked around to the opposite side of the table and Juliana met me there. She leaned in close to me, her arm looping through mine. Then brushing her mouth to my ear, she whispered, "What in the world was that?"

"Did you want this gravy now, Will?" Royce whisked the mixture in his pot, this time glancing over to Dad.

"Now." Dad waved his hands, shooing Juliana and me. "You girls go relax in the living room."

"Dad," Juliana groaned.

"It's your birthday!" I bellowed. "*You're* supposed to be relaxing." But then, he did this every year.

Juliana had moved out nine years ago. He'd been alone for nine years, and as we left for school we'd become so busy with our lives that we rarely made it home, both of us together, anyway. Juliana and I would tag team instead of having a big family visit. Once Neal and I broke up, I didn't want Dad to see me. I knew how I looked, I'm not blind. I didn't want him upset. So, for months, I left the daddy-daughter time to Juliana—who didn't have enough time in the day to accomplish everything on her plate.

It wasn't fair. It wasn't right. But I hadn't wanted him worrying over me. Not with the "P" word looming over his head. He was still in stage two of Parkinson's and so far the effects had been minimal. What would seeing me all weak and haggard do to him? I feared it would spiral him into the next stage.

"Where did you meet this guy?" Juliana set one hand to her hip, her long platinum hair swinging as she leaned to peek into the kitchen. "I like him."

I cleared my throat, trying not to choke. "He's just a friend, Jewels. I met him through work. Remember?"

"Oh right." Her body seemed to still. "Wait, this is the *Cherry Festival* guy?"

"Yeah? So?"

"Nothing." But her porcelain skin seemed to pale.

"What?" I said, smacking her arm.

Regaining her composure, she shook her head. "Nothing. I just —I don't know if it's a great idea to get involved with a client."

"Ha!" I barked, pointing a finger at her. "Hypocrite!"

"Am not!" she said, shoving my shoulder. This house truly turned us into preteens again.

"Jack," I sang, throwing up my arms.

Her eyes widened a little. "I'm not seeing Jack."

"But you are a little."

"I am not." But she sounded too defensive.

"Fine, then you want to see him." I threw out accusations, just attempting to steer the conversations away from me and Royce.

She quieted too quickly though—no comebacks.

"Jewels?"

She nibbled on her thumbnail. "You might be right."

"For reals? I was just— What do you mean I might be right?"

She slumped onto the couch. "I don't have time to date, Blake." She stared out into space, at nothing. "I don't even have enough time to be the sister and daughter I should be."

"Oh, shut up. You're fine." But I didn't see her like I once had. Still, being the older sister, my instincts to play the mom card kicked in. My insides needed to validate and comfort. Juliana was the kindest person, she was also the most driven. Sometimes the two clashed.

"I'm not the sister I should be and you know it. How in the world would I ever add another person into my life? He would just be someone I'd end up neglecting."

Part of me wanted to yell—*don't do it! Men are evil! You'll only get hurt.* But with her forlorn face—I couldn't. "You just have to decide what your priorities are."

Her brows cinched. "I've worked so hard to get where I am. I—" She shook her head. "I just don't know how to do that. How is anything but work my priority?"

I wrapped one arm around her. Gosh, when was the last time I comforted *her*? I'd been such a mess for the last year, I hadn't helped anyone, but myself—well, I hadn't really helped myself either. "There isn't a right or wrong answer. You just need to be fair to yourself and decide what you want most."

Turning her head, she peered at me with suspicion. "Why aren't you telling me that men are of the devil?"

I scratched my chin, my shoulders drooping. "Honestly, I don't know."

Her eyes widened. "It's him," she hissed in a whisper, her finger jabbing toward the kitchen.

I snatched her hand, slapping it down to her knees. "It is not!"

Jewel's azure eyes bore into me, waiting for more.

"Girls," Dad called from the kitchen. "Dinner's on."

Juliana stood and reached out a hand, pulling me up from my sunken seat on Dad's brown floral couch.

We sat at Dad's round table, me between Royce and Dad. Dad had plated for each of us. In the middle of each dish, rice, on top of that a burger patty, and on top of that gravy.

"No veggies, Dad?" Juliana whined, looking at her plate as if it might produce one on its own.

"It's my birthday. I don't want to eat broccoli today."

Royce smothered a laugh.

"Eat your red meat, Jewels. It won't kill you."

"Except that it might," she said. "Kidding Dad," she added quickly. "You know I love your burger gravy."

"So, Royce, what do you do?" Dad asked, taking a bite of food, with only the slightest tremor in his hands. I'm guessing only Juliana and I would notice.

"Yes," my sister said, her tone strangely unfriendly, "what do you do?"

"I'm a designer," he said.

"Like Jewels?" Dad asked, his tone delightful and pleased. "All you young people are so creative."

"No, not quite like Juliana." Royce smiled, another bite from his dinner hovering near his mouth, waiting on his fork. "I'm a web designer."

"A web designer?" I said, staring blankly at him. I blinked, long and slow. "But you said you worked for the *Cherry Festival.*"

"I do." He nodded, taking his bite.

"I'm confused," I said, not even attempting to hide my agitation.

"Oh boy," Juliana mumbled under her breath, while our dad just watched the showdown.

"I designed the website for the festival events. When I told them I'd heard of a great baker, they asked me to head that up as well."

I narrowed my eyes. "That's... weird."

He shrugged one shoulder as if it were no big deal. "Maybe a little. But they trust my opinion."

"A web designer? So on the computer?" Dad asked.

"Yeah. I can't wait to get a story up about Blake and the cake she'll be making. It's going to be huge." Royce winked at me, ignoring my clear agitation.

"Story?" Juliana and I said the word at the same time.

"You're writing a story on Blakeberry?" Dad beamed—always so proud of his girls.

"Well, I'm not a writer, someone else will be doing that. But I'm designing the page for the story." He dabbed his mouth with a napkin and lay the cloth on his lap.

I blinked, unsure how I felt about all this. "You never mentioned a story," I said.

"It's a new idea."

"And a great one." Juliana's strange discomfort had vanished. "Blake, this could put you on the map. You could open your own shop. You've always wanted to."

"Her own shop?" Dad clapped. "You might be my hero, Royce."

"To open a shop, you need revenue—something I don't have, remember? Let's not jump the gun. I haven't even baked the festival cake yet." I tossed my napkin next to my uneaten hamburger gravy plate and stood. "Sorry, Daddy. Excuse me... I... I need to use the restroom."

CHAPTER TWENTY-ONE

Royce

*A*fter twenty minutes of small talk, eating, and no Blake returning, I wiped my mouth with my napkin and smiled at Blake's father and sister. "Uh, I'm going to find that second bathroom you mentioned."

"Sure," Will Minola said, his eyes slipping to his younger daughter. I could see it in his face, he wished Blake would come back. He just wanted an evening with his daughters.

I stood from the table and slipped into the living room with zero intentions of using the bathroom.

"Hey!" a whisper stopped me in my tracks. I turned to find Juliana in the room, slouching as if sneaking around. "What do you think you're doing?"

"I was—"

"You're here. On a *date*. With my sister. How many others have there been?"

"Well," I scrunched my brows, "none. She keeps turning me down."

"You were supposed to boost her spirits with this job, that's it."

"And... I'm doing that. Err—at least I'm trying. I like Blake, okay?" It wasn't a lie. Somehow, someway, I had learned to like Blake Minola in the last three weeks. My left eye twitched—it wasn't the whole truth either.

Juliana stood taller. "Hmm... Okay." She tilted her head. "Just FYI, you hurt her and I come at you with a pitch ax."

I cleared my throat. "A pitch ax, really?"

She smiled at me. *"Really."* She pointed to the stairs entrance in the hallway. "She's gone to her childhood bedroom."

"Right." I mimicked her point to the stairs.

"Go on. Get her back down here. It's my father's birthday!"

"Right," I said again, then started toward the stairs.

A sitting room opened at the top of the stairs, with a door to the west and a door to the north. One had a sign on the front in curvy letters that read: Juliana. The other had a sheet of white copy paper, with black block letters saying: KEEP OUT.

I smirked. I wouldn't have needed Juliana's name to be attached to a door to figure out which one belonged to Blake.

I tapped on the door, but didn't want to give her the opportunity to send me away—so I walked inside right after announcing myself with the tap.

Blake lay on her bed, bigger than a twin, but not quite a queen. A black and white stuffed animal lay on her stomach, her arms wrapped around it. She stared at her ceiling, flicking her gaze to me for only a brief second.

"We don't have to write the story if you don't want to."

She answered with zero disdain in her tone, surprising me, "I want to."

"Oh, okay." My brows rose and I walked farther into the room. "I didn't know. You seemed unsure." I looked about Blake's large childhood bedroom. Band posters lined one wall, a desk and a dresser with trinkets atop it sat on the adjacent wall. A few photos without frames lined the mirror above her dresser. The photos showed Blake and Juliana, arm in arm, at various ages. Then, both girls next to their dad. Also, a few snapshots of teenage girls, who must have been high school friends, all standing next to a brace-faced Blake. She had one solo picture of herself, at maybe twelve or thirteen in a white chef's hat. I looked again, trying to find one of Blake with her mom—but nothing.

"Where's your mom, Blake?" I couldn't help it. Invasive or not, I wanted to know.

She tossed the stuffed animal onto the floor and scooched from the middle of her bed to the right side. I took it as some sort of invitation. She could push me off if I'd gotten it wrong. I lay down next to her, a few centimeters separating our supine bodies.

"I don't know where she is."

I slid my gaze to the side, to see a tear fall from the corner of her eye down into the mess of brown hair she lay upon. My forehead wrinkled in worry, but I looked back up at Blake's ceiling, decorated in iridescent stars.

"She left a long time ago, just after my eighth birthday."

My heart hurt a little. Sure, my parents had divorced, but they both still wanted to be in my life and in my sister's life. For the most part, they'd stayed civil for us—even when they didn't want to. I stretched out my fingers, hoping hers were close. I touched her soft skin and when she didn't pull away, I grazed further, lacing my fingers with hers.

She turned her head to look at me, her brows knit in question.

But I only said, "Go on." Then looked back to the stars.

"I thought maybe I'd done something wrong, asked for too many gifts, tried her patience, or been a bother." She sniffed, but I didn't see another tear fall.

"What about Juliana or your dad? You just went right to blaming yourself?"

"Juliana has always been sweet. I knew she couldn't be the cause. And Dad, Dad loved all of us so fiercely, why would anyone want to leave that?" She breathed out a sigh. "No, the only thing that made sense was me. I'd done something."

"Blake," I said, my tone hushed.

"Well, that's what I thought then. At eight... and at sixteen."

"And now?"

"Now, I can see she was selfish. She took the easy way out, serving only herself."

"Have you talked to her?"

"Not once," she said and her jaw clenched.

"Maybe," I said, squeezing her fingers, "maybe she had a mental health issue that wouldn't let her be the mother she should have been."

Her eyes focused on the stars above us. "Maybe. But then, that would take away all my reasons to be angry. So, until she does contact us, until I know that, I'll just believe what I believe."

"Fair enough." I ran my thumb over the length of her pointer finger. "What about Neal?"

Her hand stilled, going clammy inside of mine. "He left too. That seems to be my trend. He found someone better and didn't bother breaking up with me before he went after her." She blew out an exhausted breath, but this only made another tear fall and then a third traced the second.

"Just because he left you, doesn't mean he'd found someone better."

"Oh yeah?" she said with mocking humor.

"Yes," I don't know why, but I needed her to understand. "He left. He did it. That action says nothing about you and everything about him."

She turned her head, peering at me, more tears making her honey eyes glisten.

"He is a spineless coward."

Her pretty full lips turned up on the right side. "*Spineless.*"

I looked at her, strings of long chestnut hair splayed across her face. I took my free hand and scooped her straying hairs behind one ear. "Relationships end. It happens. But to leave with deception and lies is spineless." I swallowed, thinking of the lies that made up the root of our friendship.

She watched me for a minute. "You smell like mint, like the old peppermint gum my grandfather used to chew."

A laugh rumbled in my chest. I breathed in. "Yeah?" I said, taking in every inch of her—her glistening eyes, her pouty lips, her pink cheeks—all while she stared intently back at me. "Well, you smell like cake," I said.

"Do I?" Her smile widened.

"Yeah." I slid my gaze to her mouth, then back to her eyes. "And it just might be the best smell in all the world."

She blinked, her mouth widening into a full grin. Her lashes fluttered as she inhaled a deep breath, then leaned in, closing the gap between us, and pecked her full lips to mine. I shut my eyes taking in the sweetness of her scent and tenderness of her lips. I moved my mouth with hers, tasting the sugar that must have clung to her skin.

CHAPTER TWENTY-TWO

Juliana

"Who is this guy? Did you know he showed up at my dad's house?" I couldn't decide if I liked Royce or not. I did—and then I didn't.

Jack sat next to me on Melanie's vintage loveseat. "He's my cousin," but he said the words too slowly.

I narrowed my gaze. "What's wrong with him?"

"Nothing," this time the word came out quick.

"Then why did you say it like that?" Without thinking, I reached for Jack's hand, squeezing it in my hold. "This isn't a game, Jack. This is my sister and she's been through a lot."

He squeezed back. "Nothing is wrong with him. He's a good guy. He helped her get the festival job and..."

"And?"

"And he felt like with her past, a date or two would be good to boost her confidence as well."

Just when I thought I might like Jack Anderson a little too

much, he gave me reasons to slug him. I yanked my hand from his. "No one said anything about romancing Blake!"

"I know. I'm sorry. But truly, I think he likes her. I've never seen him work this hard to get a date." He did look sorry, but that wouldn't help my sister.

Heat spread through my cheeks. "You think—" I began, but Melanie made her way into the room, like a hurricane taking over a space.

"Oh, Juliana," Melanie said, her red hair a shade lighter than when I last saw her. "I am so glad today works for a meeting! I was worried when you canceled on me last week."

I glanced at Jack. "I'm sorry about that. My sister needed me."

"Your sister—again? Hmmm, poor girl." Melanie made pouty lips. "You know, we worked together for a year and I never knew you had a sister."

"Sure you did," Jack said. "Juliana told us that story about camping with her dad and her sister."

Melanie squinted. "Was that the story with the wildflowers?"

"Yeah." Jack nodded.

"Well, the wildflowers were the vital part of the story. Remember? Charlotte was trying to decide between traditional roses and something more unconventional. Thank you again, Juliana, your input is always helpful."

I sighed. Jack remembered that? I only remembered talking Charlotte out of the wildflowers. They really didn't go with the rest of her motif. And clearly, that's all Melanie remembered too.

"Shall we get back to business?" Melanie asked, forgetting my sister—again.

"Please." I crossed my legs.

"Next month is Charlotte and Eric's wedding shower. We're doing a combined his and hers party. It's going to be fabulous. I'll need you to dress Charlotte, Eric, MacKenzie, Jack, and me."

"Mother," Jack said, his tone cross. "Juliana has other clients.

You can't just demand something new and ingenious on three weeks' notice."

"*I'm* her client." Melanie looked taken aback, and while I had never heard Jack speak to her that way before. It appeared she hadn't either.

"For a wedding, six months from now. Not a bridal shower."

"It's a wedding shower. And, Jackson MacKenzie, this has nothing to do with you. Besides, it doesn't have to be ingenious or even brand new." She scrunched her nose in my direction. "Just spectacular."

She'd just asked me to dress Jack—so it did have *something* to do with him. Still, I slapped a smile on my face. "I can do that. No problem."

"Juliana," Jack protested, but his mother shut him up with a glare.

"You, of course, are invited," Melanie cooed. "Just make sure you bring a date." Her lashes fluttered. "Or you can attend with Jackie." She grinned. "That would be perfect."

Jack shut his eyes. She really didn't do him any favors. Couldn't she see that?

"Mother," he groaned.

"It'll get your mind of the stresses of life," Melanie said, ignoring Jack. Her mouth turned to a pout. "Your darling sister and such things."

"I don't know, Melanie. When I was young," I said, my eyes on Jack, "my father used to tell Blake and me that we wouldn't be happy unless our sister was happy. He wanted us to think of the other before ourselves. He even went so far to say that if Blake wasn't dating then neither could I." I laughed. But I wasn't joking. I'd told the story for the sake of the conversation that Melanie had cut off and for what she insinuated—that I should lose myself at a party while Blake suffered.

Melanie tittered with me but looked a little disturbed and thor-

oughly confused. Jack may have been two years older than Charlotte, but she'd never deny Charlotte anything because of that.

"Silly, maybe. It always stuck with me, though. I can't imagine
feeling complete while Blake is stuck and unhappy."

So, maybe I'd attend this wedding shower. *Maybe*—if my sister's
life progressed, if she could finally be happy. I wanted my sister
moving forward and Jack had promised to help me with that.
Although his cousin Royce made me nervous, he did seem to make
my sister smile.

And a smile from Blake was rare these days.

CHAPTER TWENTY-THREE

Blake

*M*y cell buzzed—on a Saturday morning. At nine a.m. on a Saturday morning! Ugh. "Juliana!" I groaned. Who else could it be? Who else would be up and about and bothering me so early?

With my face still in my down pillow, I poked the screen with my finger until the ringing stopped. I wasn't sure if I'd hit answer or end. I didn't care.

But then, "Hello? Blake?"

I leapt upward, on my knees, eyes wide. But the man saying hello—was inside my phone, not my apartment.

I grappled for the cell on my nightstand and stared at the jumble of numbers on my screen. "Um, hello?"

"There you are. Hey, it's Royce."

"Royce? How'd you get my number?"

"Christian gave it to me."

"Oh-kay." I nibbled on my bottom lip, remembering the way his had felt on mine.

"So," he said, interrupting my thoughts, "I've spent the last day and a half dreaming about that pistachio cake."

I laughed, then covered my mouth with my hand, as if my chuckle might give something away.

"Do you share recipes?"

"Only if you don't want to live long."

He hissed. "I was afraid it was something like that. In that case, what do you say to a walk and the best churros in the city."

I sat back on my bottom, looking down at my phone screen. "I've never made a churro."

"Which is why I've had to go somewhere else to find the best ones."

I rolled my eyes and snorted out a laugh.

"What do you say?"

"Um." I peered around my messy bedroom. A bag of Cheetos sat on my tall dresser, next to the remote. Breakfast and Netflix waited for me. "Sure. Okay." Breakfast and Netflix would be here when I got back.

"I'll text you the address."

I bit my cheek. "Okay."

"See you in an hour."

One hour. Sure, I wasn't Jewels. I could be ready in an hour. I didn't need to doll up for a churro… I focused on the clock on my phone, 9:32 a.m… at 10:30 in the morning.

One more glance at my phone told me it would be a pretty lovely spring day at sixty-five degrees. Perfect for my skinny jeans and a sweatshirt. I refused to primp or wear a scratchy blouse simply because I had kissed Royce Valentine. I mean, sure, I would be applying mascara and lip gloss, but that wasn't totally abnormal.

I showered but didn't have the time to wash my thick hair—not unless I wanted it to be damp the rest of the day. So, I opted for dry shampoo and combed through the long tresses of my brunette head.

I ordered an Uber, then my eyes shifted to my baseball cap… I picked it up, then set it back down. My hair looked good—but then, did I want it to look good? Did I care if Royce noticed it looking good?

I smacked myself in the forehead. What was wrong with me? One little kiss and I'd broke. Except—it *was* a pretty good kiss, like the kind you accidentally dream about. And then we'd eaten cake with my dad and Royce might have enjoyed my dad's favorite concoction even more than he did. He'd made such a fuss. It made me roll my eyes and grin all at the same time.

It was sweet...

In a totally stupid way.

I grabbed the cap and smashed it onto my head, then locked up my apartment and ran downstairs to meet my Uber.

Twenty minutes later, my driver pulled his mini cooper, with me squished in the back, up to the curb of the address Royce had sent me. Royce waited on the corner of the street for my arrival. I nibbled on my bottom lip and he smiled at the approaching car. Yanking off my cap, I shoved it into my crossover bag, smashing it down until it fit inside the purse. I ran my fingers through my hair before hopping out of the car to greet him.

Somehow, I didn't see the huge Ferris wheel behind Royce until he pointed it out.

"Ta-da!" he sang, his arms out.

My brows cinched. "Elitch Gardens?" I hadn't been to the Colorado theme park since Juliana and I were in school. "Is it even opened?"

"Sure. It's May."

I wasn't sure when the park opened. I never paid much attention. "You said a walk and a churro."

He shot a thumb over his shoulder toward the park. "This place has the best churros. And you have to walk—a lot."

I smirked. "Fine. Okay." I mean, we were already there.

The park smelled like sugar, with groups of people, rides, and lines every which way.

We walked through the crowds, our arms brushing one another's. "Tell me about your family," I said as we walked—no real destination in view.

I'd called Royce, James Bond—and he'd seemed that way. No family, no friends, just a man on a mission. But he'd called Melanie Kucho his *aunt*—and he had to have parents.

"My mom, Rachel, is one of Aunt Melanie's sisters. She's an engineer in California. That's where I grew up."

"Oh yeah?" I'd just assumed he grew up here. "When did you move to Denver?"

"I moved in with my dad when I was seventeen, because Aunt Melanie had offered me a job. I worked full time for her while going to college."

"Whew," I hissed out a breath.

"Yeah. It was rough." Our legs moved in time with one another as we walked. He peeked over at me. "It's the year we don't speak of."

I smirked. Then squinting ahead and nodding, I said, "I'm pretty sure I have a year like that."

He laughed, pushing up the rim of his dark-framed glasses. "Here we are. I promised." He motioned with his hand, like a *Price is Right* model. "Churros."

I lifted my brows—maybe I'd been smelling churros the entire time. "I'm ready."

He purchased two and handed me one of the hot, fried, sugary sticks.

"And your dad?" I took a bite—crispy on the outside and soft on the inside, cinnamon and sugary goodness. "Mmm," I hummed, my fingers on my sugar coated lips, "that *is* a good churro."

"I told you." He beamed, watching me.

"Your dad?" I asked again, taking another bite, my eyes on my fried dough.

"Right. Dad. He's also an engineer. That's how he and Mom met. He lives in Salem, now."

I licked the sugar from my pointer finger. "His name?"

"Oh yeah. Um," he paused a second, then said with mocking regalness, "that would be, Royce Senior."

"You're a junior?" I don't know why it made me giggle—but it did.

"I am." His face wrinkled with a cringe, clearly, he wasn't a fan of being Royce *junior.*

"What's wrong with that?" I said through another chuckle.

"Nothing—it's just, it's not really me. I've worked really hard to be my own person, so it just doesn't feel quite right."

"Fair enough." I watched a pair of toddlers being chased by a set of parents. "So," I said, glancing over to him, "I'm guessing there won't be a Royce the third in your future."

"No. If I do have a kid, I'm going to name him something trendy, like—"

"Luke Bryan Valentine," I said, suppressing another giggle. Stifling my laughter had become more difficult than it used to be. I hadn't laughed in a long time, so I hadn't practiced pushing them down.

"Yes! I was going to say Mateo or Ezra, but Luke Bryan's even better."

I paused, pointing a finger at him. "Except that you want him to have his own identity."

Royce sucked in, a hissing noise whistling through his teeth. "Ooo, you're right, let's go with Bryan Luke Valentine."

I laughed again, popping the last bite of my sweet churro into my mouth.

Royce paused in between the spinning swings and a roller-coaster and faced me. "Good?"

"Yeah," I said, my heart pattering in my chest.

He reached out a hand and brushed his thumb over my bottom lip. His topaz eyes lingering on my mouth. "Sugar," he said.

I licked my lip, but he must have erased any trace of the sweetness.

136

Still, his hand cupped my cheek, his thumb lingering near my lips. "I like you, Blake."

I breathed out, feeling so many things I hadn't even allowed myself to even think of in this last year. Before I could come up with a response—my head wasn't sure what to say to such honesty —his face inched closer, his lips a centimeter from mine. But he paused, seeming to ask—*is this okay?* So, I ignored my indecisive head and closed the gap, breathing in the cucumber and mint that always seemed to follow him. Royce's arms wound around me and I stretched up on my toes, attempting to bring him closer, to deepen the kiss, if possible.

A whistle from someone around us dropped me to my heels, parting our breaths. I touched my fingers to my swollen lips. I leaned into Royce, too afraid to look around at our audience.

Scooping up my hand, Royce intertwined our fingers. It felt so intimate and vulnerable—which was odd for the kiss we just shared. But his hand in mine made my chest *thar-ump* with skipping heartbeats.

Royce led us to a line, away from our adoring fans and we picked up talking right where we'd left off.

"Siblings?"

"One sister. Reagan's four years older than me."

"All R's huh?"

"Yeah." He shook his head, but his eyes held humor. "My parents aren't very creative." He winked down at me and we moved up a place in line. "Reagan's married with a kid—my outrageously adorable niece, Mia. They live near my dad in Washington."

"How old is Mia?"

"She's three." His smile changed when he spoke about his niece —his love for her tender and present. "Reagan's expecting again. They don't know the gender yet, but I'll tell them I know a fantastic, Russian Roulette, gender reveal, cake artist. You know, when they're ready to find out."

I cracked a grin. "Do. I might even purposely get it right for her."

"Please don't," he said, his topaz eyes shining down at me. "That would be hilarious."

I'm not sure why my cheeks burned with a blush, but they did. I tried to reign in my blaring grin by skirting my eyes to the ground. But Royce lifted my hand tucked inside his, bringing my eyes up with our tangled fingers, and touched the back of my hand to his lips. "I hope you aren't afraid of roller coasters because I have purposely distracted you into this line."

I cinched my brows—realizing I had no idea what line we waited in. But as we were close to the front, I soon saw, booming and huge—*The Mind Eraser.* I'd never been brave enough to ride the monster coaster when Juliana and I were kids. It blasted rollers through dives and spins that looked terrifying.

But I wasn't a kid anymore and I'd learned to shove down my real feelings and put on a brave face. "Let's go," I said, not even a tremor in my voice.

CHAPTER TWENTY-FOUR

Juliana

I knocked on Blake's door once more before using my spare key and letting myself in. "Blake," I called, setting my keys in the decorative bowl, on her table, just inside the door. "Have you lost your hearing?" I had knocked, after all, and it was eleven o'clock on a Saturday. She should be awake by now—that didn't mean she was, but she should be.

If I didn't know her better, I'd wonder if someone had broken into her apartment and draped her crap all over the place.

I walked to the back of her place and into her bedroom. Her blankets were on the ground and her bed sat empty. I checked my smartwatch again, quarter after eleven.

And she wasn't here?

Where'd she go?

I pulled out my phone. I snapped a pic of her bed and typed out the words:

What's wrong with this scene?

But thinking better of it, I deleted the pic and the words. I wanted her awake. I wanted her up and moving—and it looked as though she was. I didn't want to annoy her back into bed.

My phone jingled with a ring—"Blake!" But it wasn't her.

"Try again." *Jack.*

"Hey," I said, too casual for a client, "do you know where my sister is?"

"Uhh—no. Should I?"

I looked around her room once more. "No—I just, I thought you might."

"Are we worried? I can help you look."

"No. Thanks, Jack. She's just not normally out of bed at this time."

"Okay," he said. "So, are we still meeting at that suit store downtown at noon?"

"Yeah, it's just a fitting for the shower." I held my cell to my ear, peering about Blake's room as if she might jump out and surprise me.

"I wanted to get your opinion on something—I mean, if you have time."

Did I have time? I crammed my eyes closed, Blake's messy bedroom going temporarily out of my view. "Sure."

"Great," he said, "see you soon."

I made it downtown with time to spare. I sat on the U-shaped, backless couch at Angelo's Suits staring at my phone.

I'd texted Blake and when she hadn't replied, I'd done a *find my phone* search for her.

"Elitch Gardens? That can't be right."

I sent another quick text:

> Are you really at an amusement park or did
> someone steal your phone?

"Jewels?" Jack set a hand on my elbow and I jumped up at the sound of my family nickname on his lips. "Oof, sorry," he said, apologizing as I accidentally stepped into him.

I stuffed my phone into my pocket. "Sorry, Jack. My fault."

"Still trying to get ahold of Blake?"

"Yeah. No luck." I waved off my ridiculous worry. Besides, it was time to work. "Is Eric coming?"

"He's over there," Jack pointed to his soon-to-be brother-in-law. Eric's nose scrunched as he looked through a rack of suits.

"He looks excited," I said, chuckling at his unimpressed face.

Then, as if he were a ten-year-old kid, he trudged over and slumped onto the couch, two feet from where I'd just been sitting. "Juliana," he said, sounding like that ten-year-old, "do I really have to wear a suit to my wedding shower? I'm wearing a suit to the wedding already."

"This is *your* wedding shower, Eric." Jack crossed his arms over his chest. "You get to wear whatever it is my mother tells you to wear. And she would like Juliana to dress you in a suit."

Eric chortled, lifting his head and looking at himself in the trifold mirror just opposite our cushioned bench. "Melanie's not invited to the bachelor party, right?"

Jack set a hand on Eric's shoulder. "No, she is not, my friend. You can come in nothing but boxers if you like."

"This is a black and white event," I said, "and it's dressy, but you don't *have* to wear a tux. Melanie never said *formal*."

Eric lifted one brow in interest. I spent the next half an hour showing him options—a jacket with a button-up shirt, no tie and white runners, a vest with or without the tie, and black Roberto Cavalli jeans. His eyes lit when I talked about the denim. He was sold.

"You're the best, Juliana," he said, before heading out to meet up with Charlotte.

"What about you? Any clothing reservations?" I stood in front of Jack, feeling his eyes on me. They were easy to ignore as I worked with Eric, but now, they warmed my skin like laser beams.

"I trust you."

I pulled my fabric measuring tape from my jacket pocket. I lifted his arms and he held them out for me. With our bodies just inches apart, I ran my tape along his right arm. "So, how does your cousin feel about Elitch Gardens?"

"The park?" He looked thoughtful for a minute. "I think he likes it."

"Do you think he'd take my sister there?" I asked, making a mental note of his measurements.

His brows cinched, then rose. "Yeah, actually. I think he might."

I nodded. "Well, I hope she's having fun."

"Does she seem happier to you?"

She did. But more than that, she seemed willing to move past Neal and everything that's held her back this past year. This was bigger than just a happy day, bigger than I'd hoped it could be. "I think so," I said, playing it cool and remembering my promise to him.

But he didn't bring it up. He'd pretty much taken it back right after offering the bargain. His lips turned up and his eyes watched me. "I'm glad she's doing better."

The air between us grew warm. I walked to a rack of black suit coats and pulled the size I wanted from the hanger. "Here. Try this on." I helped him into the black jacket—it fit like a glove.

"Nice," he said, turning to look in the tri-mirrors. He ran a hand over the sleeve. "That's soft." He moved his shoulders, up then down. "And comfortable."

I ran my hands over the blades of his shoulders, smoothing out the back. He faced me without request and I ran my fingers over the lapels. I blinked, moving my gaze up to his, my hands still on the chest of his jacket. "It's perfect."

"Thanks, Jewels." His breath tickled my cheek and my eyes scanned down to his rosy lips.

I cleared my throat, dropped my hands, and stepped backward. "Wear your favorite white shirt—button-up or tee will work. Just make sure it's ultra-white. Then wear those white Vans that you love so much." My mouth twitched—I knew things about him too, I could be observant.

He ran the back of his hand below his chin and smiled. "I love it."

I nodded. I did too. It fit him well—body and personality. I watched him, feeling the strangest urge to run my fingers through his thick hair.

"Jewels?"

I shook my head. What was wrong with me? "I'm—I'm so glad it works. You can rent the suit coat or I'm sure Melanie would be happy to purchase it."

"Okay." He slipped his broad shoulders from the coat and handed it back to me. "So, it's lunchtime. Ah—do you need to eat?"

I did—and yet I didn't. Getting close to Jack Anderson wasn't something I'd planned on, and frankly, it frightened me a little. "I have a dozen sketches I need to create for Amy Allen by Monday. I really should get back to the office."

"On a Saturday?"

I swallowed, nodded, and avoided the piercing of his hazel eyes. "And a Sunday. I'll be there tomorrow too." I shrugged as if it were all out of my control, none of it could be helped. That's just how it was—instead of the truth, being with Jack felt like too great a temptation, too great a distraction.

CHAPTER TWENTY-FIVE

Jack

"We're friends. A friend can drop by. A friend can bring lunch." I held tighter to the bag of sub sandwiches I'd bought. "We are friends—right?" I spoke to myself, pausing on the step just outside of Juliana's office building.

It might be locked up—it was Sunday.

If so, I'd text her.

What if she only said she'd be here today to get out of spending a meal with me? I crammed my eyes closed, my hand on the doorknob of her building. I wasn't normally the negative type. But something about my efforts with Juliana made me question my every move.

I blew out a breath. One way to find out.

I tugged on the handle of the door, expecting it to stay right in place. But the door swung open to a quiet inside.

There wasn't a secretary to meet me, but I followed the same steps as last time, hoping I could avoid Juliana's passive-aggressive assistant this time around.

There were lights lit on the third floor, but no assistant. I did pass one janitor in the hallway. I pretended to belong there, adjusting the computer bag over my shoulder, and he didn't even give me a second glance.

All good signs—I hoped.

The closed door to Juliana's office didn't dissuade me, bright lights illuminated within the room—the only lit office on her floor.

I breathed out one nervous breath and set my fist to the door, knocking.

I'm not sure I'd ever seen Juliana dressed casually—but the minute she opened the door, I knew I liked it. She wore her hair in a bun on top of her head, strings of flaxen hair falling next to her slender face, with a pencil through the ball of her bun.

"Jack!" she said, her normally soft voice loud with the empty floor. She held a hand to her stomach, her midriff bare an inch around. Her short T-shirt looked old and tattered and her sweat pants hugged her hips, just barely covering her navel.

"I figured you have to eat." I held up the bag of sub sandwiches I'd purchased.

Her fingers grabbled at the back of her neck. "I—I was gonna call for a door dash."

I ground my teeth and forced a smile, plunging on. "But you haven't yet? Now, you don't need to."

She stepped back, seeming to give in a little.

"I brought six different sandwiches. I wasn't sure what you'd want."

She licked her lips and glanced at the sketches on a work table against her wall.

"I won't stay long, Juliana. I promise. Remember yesterday—I wanted your opinion on something, but you had to go."

Her brows furrowed. "Oh, that's right." She held three fingers to her head. "I'm sorry, Jack." She seemed to ease and my nerves settled with gratitude. I wanted to get to know Juliana better, not make her uncomfortable.

"I'm truly not here to bother you." Royce probably would have called me desperate and pathetic, but I just wanted a little time with her. I couldn't explain it, but Juliana made every other woman invisible to me. She was it—*everything*—and everything in me craved to be near her.

She pursed her lips. "Just give me one—one sec, okay?"

My heart thumped. "Yeah. Of course."

She walked to her work table, slid the pencil from her bun, and added something to one of the sketches. She stood straight and turned back to face me after only a minute. "Thanks."

"Can I look?"

"Oh—ah, sure. I mean they're rough drafts and I—I don't normally—"

I hadn't expected a group sketch. There were four drafted people, resembling mannequins—a man, a woman, a boy, and a girl.

"I haven't even put color to them yet. They're—"

"It's a family." I picked up the next sketch, the same four people, but with different clothing.

She sat on a stool next to her work table and stared at the work she'd done. "Yep. *People* magazine will be shooting Amy Allen's family on Moonstone Beach in California."

I held up one sketch. "Is this a formal dress?"

Juliana nibbled on the end of her thumbnail, then dropped her hand to her side. "It is. She wanted options."

I leaned against the table, studying her work. "So… do you sew all of these or are you like an architect, you create the design and someone else does the labor?"

She breathed out a tiny laugh. "I sew. I also make patterns, cut and pin fabric—"

"Okay," I laughed, "I never doubted you could *cut* fabric. I just wondered."

"Oh, cutting the fabric is often the most difficult part. It's all

146

about the angles, the math. You get that wrong, you have no chance at sewing it together correctly."

"I'm just glad I'm not in charge." I smiled at her—she knew her craft. No one could question her passion.

"Once I create a garment, and I know I'm happy with the pattern, then I'll let construction use it to make more. If that's allowed. Sometimes, like my Andrea Leawood dress, the purpose is for it to be one-of-a-kind. It's kind of a masterpiece and only one person will wear it." She sighed, but not unhappily.

"You should secretly make two—one in your size. That way you can admire it whenever you want." I lifted my brows, teasing.

Juliana chortled, her long fingers pressing to her lips. "I should," she said as if we conspired together.

"Then send me a picture. I want to see it."

She pointed a finger at me. "I'd have to swear you to secrecy."

"I can be discrete."

She stood from her stool and walked to the couch across the room. I'd set my sub sandwiches down on the table in front of it.

"I don't know, Jack Anderson," she said. "We might have to make a blood pact." She sat down on the thin, gray cushion and pulled a sandwich wrapped in white butcher paper from the bag.

I sat next to her. "Would you settle for a pinky promise?" I held out my little finger.

She slid her long, slender finger around mine. Her long lashes hooded her baby blue eyes, looking down at our hands. "I guess that'll do." She blinked, looking up to meet my gaze.

I held to her hand, not wanting to let go, not wanting to look away from her eyes—but Juliana did both for me. She slid her hand from mine and blinking, peered down at the bag of food once more.

"So," she said, "what did you bring?"

I held up the one she'd taken from the bag. I had the girl write the name of each sandwich on the wrapping paper, so I wouldn't have to open them up to remember. "Turkey with avocado."

147

She wrinkled her nose.

I breathed out a laugh. "No turkey—"

"No avocado," she corrected.

"Okay, no avocado." I pulled another from the bag. "Farmer's—this one is a BLT with egg salad." I reached in for another. "Banh mi—"

"Ooo, that's it." She held out her hands.

"There are three more—"

She shook her head. "I don't need to hear anymore."

"All right. The lady knows what she wants."

She leaned back, unwrapping her sandwich. "In clothing—yes. In a sandwich—yes. The rest of life... yeah, that I'm not always sure about."

I snatched up the turkey. "I'm not sure I believe that."

She watched me for a second and then two. "You know what I believe?" Her gaze slid to the butcher paper wrapped sandwich in my hands. "I think, you picked turkey with avocado because you know it's the one sandwich I didn't want."

"Maybe it's my favorite," I said—but she wasn't wrong. I wanted her to have options—in case she wanted another.

"*Maybe*." She still watched me, her untouched banh mi in her hands. "But I've been paying attention. And I think you'd give up your choice for someone else's every time."

"And that's bad?"

She sat straighter, laying her lunch on the table and unwrapping the paper. "Not bad. But maybe a little too self-sacrificing."

I sat up too, resting my arms on my knees. "Don't worry, Jewels. I'm not *that* good. I won't give up *every* time." Given the option for me or someone else to love her—I'm pretty sure I'd be selfish enough to always pick myself. I honestly didn't think anyone else would do her justice. I may not be worthy of her, but I would at least die trying.

The air between us grew warm and she sat back again, putting space between us. "Can I ask you something?"

I nodded, taking a bite of my turkey sandwich.

"What is it like having *Melanie Kucho* for a mother?"

I laughed—then choked on the bite I'd taken.

"Jack!" she yelped, sitting back up, she pounded on my back.

I coughed again, then caught her hand mid-slap. "I'm okay," I said. "You just caught me off guard."

"I'm sorry," she murmured, sliding her hand, so that mine no longer clutched her wrist, but wrapped snuggly in her grasp. "I didn't mean to."

I shook my head. "Don't apologize. It's normal to wonder. But to me, Melanie is just Mom. Boring as that may sound." I shrugged once. It wasn't the first time I'd been asked this question. "She's busy. Sure, Dad tucked us in at night more often than Mom. But we knew she loved us. We knew she was working for herself, but also for our family. And although, she's a little..." I thought a minute, not wanting to call my mother crazy, "*zealous,* she means well. She knows I'm fond of you—that's why she's always... pushing."

Juliana's long nails scratched at her neck, her cheeks blooming pink.

"Sorry—I didn't mean—"

She shook her head. "No, don't. You're fine." Her eyes fluttered up to mine. "You're honest, Jack. No one can deny that."

"What about your mom?" I knew Juliana had been raised by her dad, but that didn't mean I knew any more. I could never quite figure out where Juliana's mom fit in her life. That picture felt like a mystery.

"Um, I *felt* loved—which is why it's so confusing. My mother left when I was seven. Blake was eight. My memories are gray and I'm not sure all of them are real."

"I'm sorry," I said, wanting to touch her. "Do you ever see her?"

She shook her head. "No. She left a note to Dad, but nothing for us girls. I remember her kissing my head at night—when she thought Blake and I were asleep. Blake would fall asleep reading, but I stayed up drawing and I just didn't get tired. She'd come in around ten, when I was pretending or trying to sleep, and kiss our heads. One night, she didn't come in." She cleared her throat. "Dad has pictures of the four of us. But the only sure memory I have are those kisses, that one day stopped."

"Of course, I don't know what happened. But it sounds like she loved you."

"Yeah. She still left. Mothers who love their children, don't willingly leave." She set her sandwich—only two bites taken—onto the table. "I don't like to think about it much. We never wanted for anything with my dad. I can't change what happened, but even if I could, I'd never trade him for her—*never*."

My fingers twitched with her pain. "I—Juliana, can I give you a hug?"

She laughed. "A hug?"

I shrugged one shoulder. What else could I say?

And then she nodded. "Okay."

I wrapped an arm around her shoulders and she leaned into me, wrapping one arm about my waist. I held her close, her head resting on my chest. More than a hug, I held her, with zero desire to let go. I breathed in the sweetness of her hair, brushing my chin and lips over her hairline.

We sat there a while, Juliana in my arms, when a knock sounded at her door. She sat up, tears on her cheeks. She brushed them away and stood, smoothing her gray sweatpants as if they were a straight, business skirt.

She walked to the door and opened it. "Mark?"

The African American man with dreads down his back stood an entire head taller than Juliana. "I thought I heard voices in here earlier," he said. "I hoped you'd left your light on."

"I've just been working on the Allen account." She moved out of the doorway, stepping back into the room. "My friend, Jack, brought me lunch."

I stood from my perch on the couch.

"Jack, this is my boss, Mark Zudora," she said his name with awe—like maybe it should mean something to me. "Mark, this is Jack Anderson."

"Jack," Mark held out a hand to me, leather bands slipped from his arm to around his wrist, covering a small tattoo on the inside of his wrist. "Always good to meet a friend of Juliana's."

"What are you doing here?" she asked. "Isn't Sunday, family day?"

"Yes. The kids are with Alex's mother." His eyes went wide. Then, as if to fill me in, he leaned closer and whispered, "My mother-in-law." Then, back to Juliana. "I just came in to grab some files. I'm meeting with Sandra tomorrow morning." His eyes went from Juliana to me and back again. "If you have a second, I'd love your opinion."

"Ah—" she swallowed. "Yes. Of course."

I knew our moment had passed. We sat in her office—where she worked. I couldn't fault her for wanting to do that *work*. "I was just going," I said.

She pressed her lips together. "I'll talk to you soon."

I nodded, snatched up my laptop bag and sandwich, and started for the door.

"You're bag," she said, pointing to the Zepplin sandwich bag still on her table.

"This is the only one I need," I said, holding up the turkey and avocado.

Her fingers played at the collar of her shirt. She lifted her hand in a quick wave, then turned to Mark. "How can I help?"

I walked out of her office and passed the empty secretaries desk, but paused my movement when I heard Mark say—"Jack, huh?"

"It's not what you think," Juliana answered him, a groan in her voice.

"And what am I thinking? That you've finally gotten yourself a cute little blond boyfriend."

"Yes," she said through a laugh. "That's exactly what you're thinking."

"Well, why not? He seems nice."

I liked Mark, I thought, slowly inching my way toward the exit.

"He is nice, that's not the issue."

"And the issue is?" Mark asked.

"You know better than anyone that I do not have time for a boyfriend. My mother didn't have time for the people she loved and she left them. I won't do that. It's better not to get involved."

My heart fell. Her mother? She didn't want to be like her.

"Juliana, you are not your mother, honey. You'd never do that." Mark paused, tempting me to peek around the corner to see their faces. Then he said, "Can I give you advice before I take some?" I could hear a tap—I assumed his palm on the files he held. "If you don't *make* time, Jewels, the best parts of life are going to pass you by. Don't realize one day that *all* you have is your work."

CHAPTER TWENTY-SIX

Royce

"Who says we have to break up? I mean, I made up the rules for this ploy—those rules can change, right?"

"How long are you going to talk to yourself?" Jack's voice sounded behind me.

I jolted, hitting my head on the top of the break room refrigerator. I stood straight, removed myself from the opened fridge door, and slammed it closed. "Are you spying on me?"

He crossed his arms over his chest. "I came in for a drink. It's not my fault you had your head in the fridge for ten minutes."

"It's been five. I can't decide."

Jack moved past me, opened the break room fridge up, and snatched a water bottle before closing it up again. "I'm not sure you were deciding on a drink. I hate to break it to you, but your life choices aren't in there."

"My life—I'm not making any life choices, I'm thirsty." I yanked the fridge door open again and grabbed the first drink inside the door. Blah—iced coffee.

He raised his brows. "So, you're breaking up with your drink? No, wait—you *aren't* breaking up with your drink."

I sneered down at the bottle in my hands. Coffee should never be cold. "Nah, you were right the first time. I'm breaking up with my drink." I flung the door open and shoved it back onto the shelf. Not bothering to grab anything else, I stormed from the room.

"Roy," Jack called after me. He followed me out into the open work room. "Hey, hold up."

I stalked out to my standing desk and opened my laptop—I had plenty of work to occupy my head.

"Roy. Cousin, what's up?" He stood in front of me. And for a minute I tried to ignore him.

Flicking my head up to meet his stare, I shrugged—a very non-smooth shrug. "I—I like her, okay?"

His brows furrowed. "You... like..."

"Blake!" My eyes went wide with impatience. "Blake, idiot." I ran a hand through my hair. "I like her, okay? I don't want to act like a jerk. I don't want her to break up with me." I lifted my hands, shrugged again, and dropped them to slap at my sides—like a dead fish.

Jack only smiled. "What happened to—build her confidence and then let her feel in charge by breaking things off?"

I ran a hand over my mouth and chin. "I don't like that plan anymore, okay? It's... flawed."

"Flawed?"

"Yes. It's flawed." I swallowed and ground my teeth. Maybe I *should* let Blake break things off—maybe then, the insanity inside me would disappear.

"You don't want her to break up with you? What have I missed? You guys spend a few days in a bakery together and now—"

"We went on a date. I took her to the park."

One brow lifted as if he understood something. "On Saturday?"

I nodded. "Yeah, and Sunday, we went to a Rockies game." I smiled with the memory.

"Look at that grin." Jack waggled a finger at me. "You're like a little boy."

I shook my head, already full of angst. I wouldn't let Jack upset me more. "I don't know what to say. Something happened. And I like her." *A lot.*

"Something happened? You say that like you had no control."

"Maybe I didn't." I pressed a fist to my forehead, then dropped my hand. Getting irritated with Jack wouldn't help me. "I just didn't plan on falling for her."

Jack set an elbow to my desk, his head in his hand, and laughed. "Royce Valentine, I never would have thought—"

"I *am* capable of feelings, Jack."

He walked around and sat on the lower part of my duel desk. "That's not what I meant. I'm just surprised."

"You're not alone." I'm not really sure how this happened. The night I met Blake, the night she dubbed me James Bond, I would have bet money I'd never care if I saw her again.

"Stop stressing about the plan. You like her—just go with the flow."

I swallowed, peering over at him. "Yeah?" If Saint Jack agreed— maybe it wasn't a terrible idea.

"Yeah. Try not to screw things up." He smacked me on my shoulder, then took off for his own workstation.

"Thanks, Cousin," I said to pretty much myself—he'd gone. I was a confident human being—Blake so adorably pointed that out at our first meeting—so it shouldn't be too hard to squash my nerves and embrace my new feelings. I could go with this. And I could do it without fear.

Except, a little voice in the back of my mind reminded me that my relationship with Blake started out as a big fat lie, a ploy, a manipulation… Something I'd specifically called her ex spineless for.

I swallowed and grit my teeth.

Lifting my phone, I stared at the picture I'd taken of the two of

155

us in front of Coors Field. Blake wore her baseball cap on her head and a blaring grin on her face. My left arm wrapped about her waist, hugging her close. I blinked, taking in the picture again and then again.

A lie...

And then, I squashed down that voice too.

Because none of it felt like a lie.

~

"*Y*ou won't have to do a single thing," I held my phone close, my palm sweating. "I've set everything up with the journalist."

"Yes, but this isn't your festival, Royce. Besides, you may organize this interview. You may design my site, but it's still my website." Fran couldn't be laid back—not for one single second.

"It's one link. A link on the festival page, to an entirely different page, that you aren't paying for, with a story about Blake Minola *and* the *Cherry Blossom Festival*. It's good publicity—demonstrating how much the community loves your festival, and it's free. I'm not sure why you're fighting this."

"Because, this is a committee decision, not a Royce decision. Last I checked you weren't on the committee Royce. You're our *web designer.*" Fran harumphed into the phone and I swore I could hear her pacing. "Is she even Japanese?"

Okay... I had totally been avoiding that topic. Yes, the festival's purpose was to celebrate Japanese heritage, and sure Blake was not, in fact, Japanese. I paused too long.

"That's what I thought."

"Isn't the festival also about celebrating diversity?" I said, pulling anything I could out of thin air.

"Is Blake a minority?"

"She's a woman," I said, reaching. "Aren't all women minorities? She's a woman trying to make it in a man's world. She's going to create something authentic to Japanese culture and the festival. I just want one little link sharing that. Come on Fran—you *are* that woman, making it in a man's world. Surely you can help a girl out."

The pause on her end made me want to pump my fist in victory —but it seemed a bit premature. "Fine," she groaned. "But one little link. It does not mess with any of my other content."

"Of course." I did pump my fist.

"And Royce?"

"Yes, Fran?"

"Don't ever say the words—*help a girl out*—again. You are a white male, you aren't allowed to say that. Women's oppression is real, my friend."

I cleared my throat. "Believe me when I tell you that I know I don't understand that as well as I should. But Fran, my intentions are honorable. Blake's worth it."

CHAPTER TWENTY-SEVEN

Blake

I mindlessly picked up the clothes and mess in my bedroom—something I hadn't done in months, all with my phone in one hand.

Royce texted back seconds after I'd sent him a message.

```
You're making the cake tonight? The Festival is
                  a month away.
```

I laughed. Clearly, he hadn't read my text well. My heart pattered as I wrote him back. I didn't want to like him this much—but I did. I wasn't even sure I could have stopped it. It seemed to be a power all in itself—my feelings for Royce. They grew and became something special before I even realized they were forming—before I could let my experience with Neal tell me to run away.

> Not the actual cake, dork. That's why I said
> PRACTICE. It's a practice cake.

He texted back:

> As in we get to eat it afterward? I'm in!

I giggled again—*giggled*, when was the last time I'd actually giggled? I couldn't decide if the thought delighted or annoyed me. Still, I couldn't deny I loved his enthusiasm about cake—err, *my* cake. Stupidly, it spurred my attraction for Royce Valentine all the more.

I dropped the misplaced tennis shoe in my hand to the floor, forgetting to toss it into the closet, and typed out another text.

> Great! Let's start at 7pm. I'm bringing cake,
> so you're in charge of dinner.

I typed out a kissy face emoji and then deleted it just as quick. I set the phone down on my newly cleared dresser and ran a hand over my forehead. "That was close."

But what was close? Hadn't I kissed Royce a few times now —*seven*, actually? We had kissed seven times. My head had decided to keep track. And every kiss got better. He held my hand—and I let him. We even took selfies together at that baseball game. Self- ies, where I couldn't have wiped the smile from my face, had I used bleach to erase it.

So why did I care about a stupid kissy face emoji?

I swallowed.

It wasn't me—that's why. And I wouldn't suddenly become someone else, just because I liked a guy.

My phone sang with an alert and I grappled to pick it up quicker than I needed to.

Royce had written me back.

Perfect.

He wrote, with a kissy face emoji.

I bit my lip, holding back my grin.

～

"That's kind of small," Royce said over my shoulder. He watched as I put my eight-inch round almond cake into the hot oven. "Isn't it?"

I snickered, focusing on my cake. "This is a sample, just an example of what I'll do. It's scaled down quite a bit."

"That makes sense." His hand found my hip and once I'd closed the oven door, he turned me around, pulling me in for a hug. His nose and mouth nestled into the crook of my neck and chills ran down my spine and into my knees and toes.

I wrapped my arms about his neck, and he slid his cheek next to mine, pulling away from my neck for kiss number eight. I stretched up on my toes, cursing my short legs, but really, long legs or not, I couldn't have pulled him any closer.

My calves gave out on me and I rocked back onto my heels.

With his hands on either side of my face, Royce's nose brushed mine. He pecked me once more—number nine—then said, "I don't want your dinner to get cold."

I pressed my enflamed lips together, suddenly starving. "What did you bring?"

"I brought," he said, his thick, russet brows bouncing, "*inspiration*." He pulled a Styrofoam container from the cardboard box he'd brought. "We've got a sushi sampler," he grabbed another, reading on top of each closed container, "hibachi chicken rice, shoyu ramen, and teppanyaki."

"Japanese take out. Nice."

"Chopsticks?" He held a pair out to me.

"Yep." I snatched them from his hands and slid them from their white wrapper.

We sat at the empty, metal counter in the back kitchen of *Much Ado About Cakes*. I didn't worry about someone interrupting us. Christian had left for the day and the shop closed at five. Gender reveals everywhere would have to wait.

Royce set a plate in front of me and then one in front of himself. He dished a small portion of everything onto each of our plates, then sat on the stool next to me.

I watched him, unable to keep my eyes from doing anything else. He made me laugh. He made me think. And he was sexy as a paperback harlequin. I swallowed, my nerves jumbling. How could I be this smitten? It made me uncomfortable. Happy—sure. Comfort—that may take a while. I'd spent the last year and a half loathing Neal and anything male.

Feeling my stare, Royce peered over at me. "What?"

I shook my head, my brows rising. "Nothing."

The warmth of his palm cupped my jaw, his fingertips at my neck. "You okay?"

I nodded in his hold and he leaned close—for kiss number ten.

&

"*W*hat's that?" Royce peered over my shoulder, pointing at my plastic mold.

"This is a mold I found online." I held it up for him to see. "See? This one here and this one?" I pointed out two of the four flowers in my plastic mold. "These are cherry blossoms."

He sat next to me, then turned and faced me so that our knees bumped into one another.

"Pay attention," I said, "You're going to help me in a minute."

He inched his stool closer, watching my hands and the mold I held.

"This," I said holding up a ball of paste, "is modeling paste. It's made of sugar and totally edible—though I wouldn't recommend eating it."

His eyes lifted to mine in question.

"Just sugar—nothing special."

"Who needs those calories," he teased.

I kneaded the paste, mixing further the two colors I'd combined earlier that day. "Right." I dusted my mold with corn flour.

"What's that?"

"Just to keep the paste from sticking to the mold."

Pinching off a small ball of the paste, I pressed it into my mold, until the paste smoothed flush with my mold. Then I popped the paste from the mold and a little cherry blossom fell onto the counter.

"Wow," Royce beamed—like a little child seeing bubbles blown for the first time. "Look at that." He picked up the blossom and examined it closer.

In minutes I had six more made. "We'll make them in batches so that I have time to paint them before they dry out completely."

"Paint?"

"Edible paint, yeah. They'll look like real flowers by the time we're finished."

Again, he watched closely as I painted the center of each flower. Then using a Dresden, I fanned out the petals of each flower, making them individual and more realistic. With paint, I brought life to each little petal.

"You ready to try?" I asked once I'd finished.

Royce grinned, holding one of my little cherry blossoms up for inspection, "you're an artist."

I shrugged. "I'm a baker." I pointed to the opposite side of the room. "Can you grab that dry foam?"

He hopped up to do my bidding while I put the final touches on a few more flowers. He set the foam piece in front of me and I placed each little flower in an already indented crevice.

"They'll dry here," I explained. "This will give them their cute little cup shape."

"And a genius. I've fallen for an artist and a genius."

I cleared my throat, a tremor in my hand making me fumble with my next flower. I dropped it haphazardly onto the foam and stood. Brushing my hands together, I marched to the sink to wash my hands, my back to him.

He talked big—just being Royce—eccentric, like always. He was—

"Hey," he said, just behind me.

I didn't turn. "Hey," I said back, scrubbing my fingers as if I might be going into surgery.

He leaned his back against the opposite side of the large commercial sink, his dark topaz eyes on my face. "Should I have not said that?"

"Said what?" My voice cracked.

"I think they're clean, Blake." Royce set a hand over top of mine, still bubbling with suds. "I didn't mean to make you uncomfortable. I thought you knew how I felt. I thought a dozen kisses later, you'd figured it out."

I pressed my lips together, so as not to correct him—ten kisses, not a dozen. I blinked, lifting my gaze to meet his. "I mean, I guessed you might like kissing me." I am allergic to being vulnerable—I must be.

He snickered. "That's accurate, yes. But I like *you*, Blake—" He swallowed, and for the briefest moment, he seemed a little uncomfortable too. "A lot," he added with a blink.

CHAPTER TWENTY-EIGHT

Juliana

*J*held my phone to my ear, frozen, waiting for more.
"Well?" I said. "What did you say back?"

"Umm—" Nothing intelligible came out of my sister's mouth.
"Blake!"

"I don't know," she bellowed back. "I just told him that I liked him too. *Duh.* I wouldn't kiss a guy unless I liked him."

"Wow." I rubbed my temple. "You've had quite the month and a half."

"I know, it's weird and—"

"No, Blake, stop. It's great. I'm—I'm really happy for you." I turned down the air blowing in my car, wanting to hear her better. I wanted to better understand what she wanted. "So, is he coming tonight?"

"To Dad's farewell dinner?" she said, a whine in her tone. "No."

"Are you sure? Because he can," I said, all the while hoping she'd stick to her *no* answer. I wanted an evening with just the three of us before Dad left for Scotland for four weeks.

"Jewels, tonight is for family."

"Right." I leaned my head back against the headrest of my seat.

"Where are you? You sound like you're—are you driving?"

"I'm stopped."

"But you're in your car?" she said, her tone inflecting with surprise.

"Yeah. So?"

"It's the middle of the day. Do you have a fitting or something?" She knew me well. I usually saved the running around parts of my job for Saturdays.

"No, not today. I'm just—" I swallowed, my mouth going dry.

"Jewels?" Blake said, accusation in her voice. "You're what?"

I huffed out a breath, remembering what Mark had said. "I'm making sure the best parts of life don't pass me by."

After a long pause, she said, "What? What does that mean?"

I threw up my hands, my phone still tucked in my right palm. "I don't know! Just something Mark said to me two days ago…and I can't get it out of my head."

"So," Blake said, a new softness in her tone, "where are you?"

I cleared my throat. "Sitting outside *The Creative Drive*."

"Where Royce works? Ohhh," she crooned, "where *Jack* works."

"Yes," I blew out a breath, "where Jack works."

"In the middle of the day?" she deadpanned.

"Yes, in the middle of the day."

"Who are you and what have you done with my sister?"

I laughed at her semi-joke. "It's me. I promise."

"Wow, Jewels. So, Jack is how you're going to make sure life doesn't pass you by?"

"No—well maybe." I looked out at the office building and my knees began to shake once more. "I think I need to stop comparing myself to mom—"

"Mom? *Juliana*," she said, her voice serious, no silliness or joking anymore. "You aren't like her."

"But I could be." I blew out a breath, repeating the voice that had been in the back of my mind, haunting me for years. "If there's nothing in my life, but work, then there's no one to disappoint. At least no one I love."

"Okay—*ouch*. I am someone. Your sister. Remember me?"

"I meant someone *else*. Someone..."

"I know," she said. "Jewels, you'd never do what mom did. Your heart is too big for that. And you don't *want* to do what she did. That means something."

I wasn't disagreeing with her. But those words had been the little devil on my shoulder—telling me it could happen, I could end up as selfish as her. They were easy to muster—still, I worked on ridding them from my brain. Because Blake was right, I didn't want to be like her—I'd made my mind up about that years ago. And Mark was right too, fear had stolen a lot of opportunities from me. I didn't want to give in to it anymore. "You're right. So, here I am trying." I blew out a breath. *Trying*.

~

I'd been to Melanie's office a hundred times. No one batted an eye at my presence. So why did I feel like such an imposter?

I walked past Royce, giving him a second glance—he'd been kissing my sister after all—and right to where Jack worked at his desk.

Fake it until you make it, Juliana—I dutifully told myself.

"Jewels," Jack said, getting to his feet. "I didn't know you had a meeting with my mom today."

I set a hand to my hip and shrugged one shoulder. "I don't. I'm here to see you."

"Me?" He ran a hand through his ash blond hair, his blue-green eyes flicking from me to the work at his station.

My cool demeanor faltered. "Is it a bad time?"

"Nope," he stammered, smiling so wide I could have counted his white teeth.

I didn't want to stay at *The Creative Drive*, though. "I owe you a lunch. Are you up for it?"

His eyes glimpsed down at his desk once more. "Well, yes. I have—"

"Nothing," Royce said from just behind me. "He has nothing." Then he flicked his chin at Jack. "Transfer your calls to me."

Jack's more natural smile lit his face. "I have nothing." He lifted the receiver on his office phone, pressed a few buttons, and set it back down. "Where are we going?"

I pointed back at his laptop. "Bring your computer. I never got to check out the site you wanted to show me."

He picked up his bag and followed me outside.

"I can drive," I told him, pointing to my silver Mazda. "Are you in the mood for an incredibly greasy burger?"

He laughed, looking me over. "Um, are you?"

"I'm thinking about French Fries and a salad."

He smirked. "Let's go then."

We sat side by side at the diner, a plate of fries between us, our heads together as we looked at Jack's computer.

"I want to highlight the designer, and showcasing her work seems the best way to do that. There is a picture of her down here." He scrolled to the bottom of the page and pointed to a black a white photo of a woman maybe a decade my senior. "I guess my question is—if this were your site, would you want your photo up front?"

"Hey, hey," I said, setting a hand on his to stop his back and forth scrolling. A vibration ran up my arm with his touch, but I ignored it. "You're scrolling too fast. Let me see."

He set his hand on the table and I took over the mouse.

"Jack," I said, truly impressed, "this is beautiful."

I could feel his gaze on me, but I kept scrolling.

"It's fashionable, yet functional. The pop of color here," I pointed to the screen, "and here, are fantastic."

He grinned. "And her photo?"

"Leave it. Exactly where it is." I set my fingers to the keys and typed in my own web address. "Look at this," I said, sitting up, giving him a full view of the screen.

"Is this your site?" He glimpsed at me, but only for a second, and then his eyes studied the website I built myself.

"It is."

"This is great."

"Something isn't right though." I looked more pointedly at him. "Right?" I hadn't planned to put him to work, but then I hadn't planned to be so inspired by his work.

Without reservation, Jack took the mouse from my control. He pointed to the screen. "See this? This is your brand. You always want to start with that. Then give them an option, a link to products or opportunities." He scrolled down. "You've got examples, but they're down here, show them earlier," he clicked, "and make them a button. When I click on these pants, I want to see more... pants."

"Okay, so brand first, then a button?"

"Yeah, a button for everything you want to showcase. Your more specific options should be right below that." His eyes turned to slits, squinting, studying the screen and he looked so adorably intense. "Do you have a review? I know my mom would write one—or Amy Allen? Having a recommendation by someone of their status, here or even here," he pointed to the screen again, "would really be valuable too."

An hour later, we'd closed the laptop and I had a dozen unexpected ideas for my site. Jack and I still sat on the same booth bench, but our French fries were long gone. His elbow rested on the back of the booth, his hand against his head, and he faced me.

"Which finger?" I asked him, after a story about Royce breaking Jack's finger when they were kids playing softball.

He stretched out his right hand, wiggling his pointer finger. "This one."

I took his hand in my hold and traced the finger he indicated. "At least it wasn't your ring finger." I'd never paid attention to his misshapen finger before.

"Jewels, it's my typing finger," he said, his tone playful as he attempted to milk more sympathy.

"You don't type with all ten?" I quirked one brow, moving my eyes from his hand to his face.

He breathed out. "Just this one."

I laughed, but I didn't drop his hand. I kept it in my hold, in my examination for a minute longer and then another minute. My chest hammered on the inside with my deliberate action. Jack's soft, strong hands felt right. Swallowing, I laced my fingers through his. Then, I examined his fingers intertwined with mine. Returning my gaze to his hazel eyes, I said, "That's a shame."

He studied me more closely. He hadn't missed my smooth move—though I acted as if it were perfectly normal for me to hold his hand.

"So, am I allowed to hire you while... we're on a... date? I'd love more help with my site."

"A date?" His brows raised. Had I not made that clear? Probably not, with my nerves going crazy.

"I thought maybe this counted as—"

"You don't have to fulfill that stupid bargain, Jewels. I hope we've helped your sister, that's all."

I cleared my throat. Why was this so difficult? Jack had already said he wanted to date me. Why did saying that back feel like climbing Mount Everest? I wanted to try. "I'm not doing this because you helped Blake. I'm here because I want to be." My eyes shifted to the table, to the lifeless laptop.

"Really?" He dipped his head, finding my eyes once more.

I swallowed, my nerves rising. "I mean, I'm not going to

169

suddenly be free from work, but if you're willing to be patient with me, I'd like to take time to get to know you better, Jack."

Jack pressed his free hand to my cheek, cupping my jaw and peering intently into my eyes. Skin against skin—I warmed where he touched. "Can I have Saturday?" he asked as if asking for a crumb from a loaf of bread.

"How about tonight instead?" I said, offering him a slice.

~

"Make sure you keep your phone on you." I pointed a finger at my father.

"At all times," Blake added. "And send pictures!"

"And no pubs!" I cleared away our dinner dishes, mentally going through my list of do's and don'ts for Dad.

"Wait," he and Blake said at the same time.

"Jewels, it's Scotland. He has to go into a pub." My sister moaned as if I were denying her Christmas.

Dad pointed a finger at her. It tremored only a bit, but it still reminded us that he wasn't exactly whole right now. What if he needed us and we weren't there?

"They're dangerous!" I threw out my arms.

"They're not. I'll be safe, my little worrier."

I sighed, but couldn't argue with his broad smile and sincerity. He was finally doing it—going to Scotland. Seeing a part of the world he'd always dreamt about. "I'm proud of you, Dad." I set the dish in my hand on the counter and walked to where he sat. Pressing my cheek to the top of his thick salt and pepper head, I hugged him.

"Hey!" Blake protested. "Me too! I'm proud too."

Dad and I each held out an arm and the three of us embraced. We hadn't had a *snuggler* since Blake and I both left for college, leaving Dad an empty nester.

"All right, who wants dessert?" I stood straight, brushing a straying tear from my cheek.

"Dessert, we just ate." Blake pressed a hand to her flat tummy.

I scratched the back of my neck and lifted my arm to see my watch.

"Where are you going?" Blake said, her eyes on me. "What's your hurry?"

My hurry? I'd double booked my night. I went from all work to dinner plans with family and evening plans with Jack. Ugh. Would I never learn balance? I didn't feel like throwing myself under the bus, though. "Hey Dad, has Blake told you she has a *boyfriend*?"

My dad's brows rose, his wide eyes on my sister.

She smacked my shoulder with the back of her hand, but said, "I made whiskey caramel cake, Dad! Let me cut you a slice." Charging into the kitchen, Blake hurried our night along—without any help from me.

I grinned across the table at Dad.

"Well, that's something I haven't seen in a while."

I turned my head toward the kitchen. "I think she's happy. She's doing so much better."

He reached across the table for my hand. He snatched hold of a couple of my fingers and shook. "No, I meant *that* grin." He nodded toward me. "My carefree Juliana joy. I'm glad it's back."

I swallowed, I hadn't known I would change with one little freeing decision. But I had. And Dad could see it too.

CHAPTER TWENTY-NINE

Jack

Juliana stared at me, sitting on her gray-ashen couch. She tried to look serious. She tried not to let the smile tickling at her lips come alive—but I could see it. "It's pretty bad when I am the one lecturing you to put away work," she said.

"I know. I just want to show you one template. One." I waved her over, my computer already opened. I'd worked the entire afternoon and couldn't wait to show Juliana the fruits of my effort. "Work with me for five minutes and then I promise I'll put it away."

Carrying the glasses of pink lemonade she'd made, she walked over to the couch. She set each glass on a coaster atop her white square coffee table. "I thought we were watching a movie," she teased—glancing at the door just behind me. She'd already given herself away and told me that her Amy Allen sketches sat waiting in her home office. But she was trying—really and truly trying to make time for something other than work. Time for me. And I hoped one day, for us.

Yet here I sat, asking her to look at website templates. To *work.* "We will, I promise." I patted the seat next to me, ready for her to be close. "I can't wait to watch," I peered up at the television, searching for the title of the movie she'd chosen, "Love on the Rocks."

She smirked, then sat next to me, her leg touching mine. This woman took my breath away in ripped jeans, a plain white T-shirt, and barefoot. Seriously... I never had a chance.

"You did all this today?" She scrolled through my work on her website, her teasing gone, her interest peaked.

"Yeah. I had time."

"Not likely. I am certain you had something better to do! A client more pressing," she said, and her long hair fell over her shoulder.

"I didn't." I mean, I could have... but I'd prioritized.

Her lips curved to a grin and she pointed at the screen. "Could we switch out this green, brighten it up a bit?"

"Of course."

"How soon can we launch it?" she asked, the glow from my computer lighting up her face.

"I can have it up and running in a couple days."

She leaned back, eyes still on the computer. She nibbled on her bottom lip and I wondered if she wanted me to change something else, but didn't dare ask. "Jack, remember earlier when I asked if we were allowed to talk about work while on a date?"

"Yes—that's when you informed me that we were on a date." I grinned, suppressing a laugh. "It was a pleasant surprise." Had it really only been this morning?

"Right." She blinked, her long dark lashes looking shy as she lifted her gaze from the laptop to me. "I have another question." She stared, her eyes skirting from my eyes to my chin and back again. "Am I allowed to kiss you while we're working?"

I gulped but stopped myself from choking. Then, smacking the laptop closed, I stretched my arm out across the back of the couch. I hadn't expected that from Juliana. Wanted it—*oh yeah*. But I hadn't allowed myself to believe it might be a reality just yet. "Ah—yes." I didn't have any of Royce's smoothness—I never would.

Even without any coolness on my end, she moved into the crook of my outstretched arm, her head nestling on my shoulder as if it were made for her. I think maybe it had been. "When I was a girl," she said, "my dad told me I could be anything in this world. I never doubted him. I always believed him. He was so earnest." Her body hugged at my side, and she set a hand to my chest, peering up at me.

"Could you be with me?" It left my mouth before I thought about the words. They just came—natural and honest.

Could she? Could she be the up and coming; the new and fresh; the sought-after Juliana Minola, fashion designer extraordinaire, *and mine*?

She lifted her chin in answer. I brought my head down just inches to meet hers. And then, I kissed her, like I'd wanted to do every day, for the last twelve months.

CHAPTER THIRTY

Royce

"Jack," I said, pointing at Clarisse, our office manager. "Have you seen Jack?"

She nibbled on the yellow body of a number two pencil. "Recording room," she said, her eyes never leaving her computer screen.

With our open office design at *The Creative Drive*, we had to have places where people could go to be alone—three conference rooms and one recording room. Lucky me—Jack already occupied one. I needed to talk to my cousin, and I needed to do it without the prying eyes of our coworkers.

The red light outside the windowless recording room shone brightly, meaning—*do not disturb*. But I didn't care. Jack could restart whatever video or vlog or screencast he worked on. I needed to talk.

Ignoring the stop light, I pushed open the unlocked door.

"Here you'll see—" Jack paused, his brows knit in confusion as he looked up at me.

"I have to tell her," I said.

"Tell... who? What?" His eyes slid from me to his waiting recording.

"Blake," I barked, my tone unforgiving. I blamed Jack for my predicament—he'd gotten me into this! He was the only other person who knew. So, he had to listen to me—whether he wanted to or not.

He glanced at his screen again.

"What are you doing?" I threw out a hand as if it were absurd for him to be working—*at work*.

"Just a screencast for Juliana's new website."

I scratched my head and narrowed my gaze at him. "Things are going... well?"

He stood and walked out from behind the single desk in the room, leaning against the edge of it. "Very."

I nodded, glad for my cousin, but that didn't clean up my royal mess. I ran a hand through my carefully managed hair. "I gotta tell her, Jack. The truth."

Jack's eyes darted from the floor to my face, thinking. "Ahh—I've never been one to condone lying, but... are you sure that's a good idea?"

I shrugged. I paced the ten feet width of the room. "No. I'm not sure of anything anymore. It's just lying to her—I mean, I'm not, not really. Everything has been *real*. Yet there's this thing..." that stupid bargain, "hanging over my head. And," I blew out a tired breath, "I don't think I can live with that. She has to know the truth." However, the sad truth was—without that stupid bargain I never would have worked so hard to ask Blake out. I hated and loved the deal all at once.

Jack watched me walk—back then forth. "So... tell her," he said, but the words sounded more like a question.

I stopped walking, my breathing heavy like I'd just run a marathon. "People who fall in love are gluttons for punishment. Were this any other guy, I'd tell him to keep his mouth shut. Why get in trouble over nothing?" I shrugged, slapping my arms against my side. "So, why do I feel compelled to be truthful with her? Why can't I just leave it alone?"

"Well," he said, dipping his head and looking at me as if I might break—a look that made me want to break him—"It sounds like you love her."

I blinked. I ground my teeth. I wanted to deny it. "It's been two months since we met, Jack."

"Yep," he said, as if my defense meant nothing. And maybe it didn't, because I couldn't deny what he said.

"When did I turn into a glutton?" I muttered under my breath.

"So you admit that you love Blake?" His brows lifted as if this were a counseling session and I'd just had an enormous break-through.

"I... admit that I'm a glutton." I turned for the door but didn't open it. Inside I twisted around and pointed a finger at my cousin —who wasn't talking me out of this crazy idea. "This isn't going to end well."

"You don't know that."

"I do. I know Blake. She won't forgive me." Sweat pooled at my forehead and I ran another hand over my head, snagging on a fistful of hair. "I wouldn't forgive me."

Jack tilted his head, trying to keep eye contact. "But you're still going to tell her?"

I brushed my fist over my chin, thinking. My whole body rejected the idea. "I am." I blew out a breath, my chest bursting with pain. "I have to. She means too much. She deserves to know." I set my hand to the doorknob of the recording room. I craved her kiss, her touch, her smile, and after today—I'd never have them again.

"When? Will you at least wait until after the festival?"

I didn't want to ruin the *Cherry Blossom Festival* for Blake... but could I wait three more weeks? "I don't know."

"What changes if you wait?"

"Three more weeks of fueled hatred?" I shrugged, turning around and letting go of the exit.

"You're so sure she'll hate you. Maybe she'll thank you for believing in her, for giving her a chance to make something so beautiful."

I shut my eyes and slid a hand down the front of my face. "I don't think she'll see it that way."

"But you don't know."

"I'll think about it." My gut ached with guilt. If I waited three weeks, I might die of pain. I left Jack alone to make his screencast, and to be alone myself. I needed to think about what I should do. I knew I had to tell her, but when?

Selfishly, I wanted to see that cake almost as much as Blake wanted to make it. I snuck away into the men's restroom. Bending over the sink, I splashed water onto my face. *She wanted to make it...* She wanted to make that cake more than anything. I knew that without a doubt. Okay, then.

I wouldn't take that from her.

CHAPTER THIRTY-ONE

Blake

"Is he going to take pictures?" Juliana spoke to me through the speakerphone of my cell. It laid on the metal counter out front of *Much Ado About Cakes* while I crafted hundreds of perfect—yet individual cherry blossoms for my cake.

"I have no idea."

"But you brought clothes to change into?"

I glared at my cell as if it were Juliana's face. "No, I didn't bring clothes." I scoffed. "The Festival is in two weeks. I am making hundreds of intricate cherry blossoms. Not to mention I have three gender reveals and one birthday cake scheduled this week." I did not have time to worry about clothing. "I'm a baker. Aren't my baking clothes good enough?"

"Blake," she scolded, "this is your first interview. This is huge. This interview could mean you never make another gender reveal ever again." She dropped the words like a bomb, then went quiet.

I paused my work, thinking.

The pink and white of the little flowers I'd been working on for hours came in and out of focus. No more gender reveals? "Fine," I said, "bring me some clothes."

"Yes!" Juliana cheered.

The front door of the shop opened and Royce stood just inside, watching me with a lop-sided grin.

"Jewels, gotta go. See you in an hour."

I hit end on my phone and brushed the corn flour from my hands. "Hey," I said, my heart pattering at the sight of him. Did I feel this way with Neal... I couldn't remember.

"You ready?" He walked closer, while I came out from behind the counter to meet him.

"I think so. I made another sample cake—to show the journalist." I shot my thumb over my shoulder at the eight-inch round I'd made as a mini example of the real thing.

He shoved his hands into the pockets of his jeans. "That's even prettier than the last one." He stood directly in front of me, his eyes still on my cake. "I wonder if it will taste better too?" His serious tone cracked and his perfect lips turned up.

I smacked his chest playfully. "You can eat it after the interview. I promise."

Royce laughed. "Deal." Pulling one hand from his pocket he pointed at my little masterpiece. "You should let the journalist try it."

"You think?" I turned, standing side by side next to him, looking at my cake as if it were a child, and I, its mother.

"Absolutely, Blake. No doubt he'll be impressed, but let him taste it and he'll be enlightened."

I smirked. "Enlightened?"

"Yes." His fingers slipped around mine. "I was." He peered down at me and suddenly our easy banter switched to pattering hearts. "I always liked you—"

"Liar."

"Okay, I was learning to like you—"

I laughed, covering my mouth with my free hand.

"Then I tried your cake, and that's when I knew," his hand cupped my cheek, and his dark eyes studied mine.

"You knew what?" I said, my voice too quiet to be normal.

"That's when I knew I couldn't live without you."

I laughed again, then shoved him in the chest, pushing him a foot away from me. "That is the cheesiest thing I've ever heard."

Royce lunged for me, "Cheesy? That was heartfelt, Blakeberry!" He scooped me about the waist and pulled me close. Lowering his face to my neck, he kissed my skin, then purposely scratched and tickled at my throat with his beard. His black frames slid from their place to the tip of his nose.

"Stop!" I giggled.

He hugged me close but stopped the torture. My hands pressed to his chest and his face dipped low, close to my own. I lifted my hand, just enough to push his glasses back in place.

"Thank you."

"You are a goofball," I said, unable to control my blaring grin.

"Probably. But I am earnest."

"Earnest?" I giggled again, my heart thumping so hard next to his chest, that he must have felt it. "Are you suddenly from 15th century England?"

He lifted one shoulder. "Does that turn you on? Because—"

I shook my head, but laced my fingers around his neck, pulling him in for kiss number… I wasn't sure anymore. I'd lost track.

His lips were soft and warm and asked me to never stop. Who needed air?

Apparently, we both did.

Still in his hold, Royce leaned down, hugging me, somehow closer, and pressing his lips and nose to my neck once more, softly this time. He breathed in the sugar that seemed to cling to my skin and clothes.

"When we first met did you ever think we'd ever be… here?" I asked. It still hit me like a hammer at times—he was *here*, this was *something*… something I hadn't expected. And something I wanted.

"No," he said so quickly, so decisively, that it made me laugh.

"Me either!" I squeezed him tighter. "I'm glad we are," I whispered, my insides feeling as if someone might be electrocuting them. The words were too honest and too vulnerable—but they made up every nerve ending in my body.

He breathed out a sigh—almost sounding sad. "Me too," he said, pressing a kiss just below my left ear. "So much."

~

*A*n hour later Juliana had dressed me in tight button-up jeans—that I had no desire to know the price of—a flowy white blouse, tucked in French style, as well as a springy striped cardigan. She talked me into four-inch, pink heels, even though I assured her no one would be looking at my feet.

At the shop door, she took one look back at me, just as a man in a dress shirt and vest, carrying a messenger bag walked inside.

Her eyes went wide and then she gave me a quick thumbs up before leaving.

"Blake Minola?" said the man.

"Yes," I said, telling myself to smile. "Cameron?"

"Yep."

"Great." I cleared my throat, my nerves rising. "Let me lock up —then no one will bother us."

"Sure."

The click-clack of my heels sounded ridiculous and it took me twice as long to reach the front. I switched the lock, my heart a train wreck, and turned back to him.

"How long have you owned the shop?" he said—unofficially, he had no notes out yet. But he looked about the room.

"Oh, I don't. Christian McKay is the owner. He's in the back if you'd like to meet him."

Cameron shook his head. "No—I just assumed." He smiled a bit awkwardly as I made my trek back to the counter where two stools waited for us. "Do most bakers wear high heels?" His mouth went lop-sided and his one brow raised above the other all while he peered down at Juliana's stupid pink heels.

"No," I said, kicking off the shoes and booting them farther beneath the counter. "My sister is a clothing designer." I shook my head. "She insisted on dressing me today." I swallowed, somehow feeling more at ease standing there barefoot. "Normally, I'm in yoga pants, a T-shirt, tennies, and an apron. It's very glamorous."

Cameron laughed. "Well, it makes sense."

We sat and Cameron pulled a notebook, as well as a recorder from his bag. "Tell me about yourself, Blake. How long have you been doing this?"

So I talked. And talked. I told Cameron about culinary school, I told him about experimenting in the kitchen when I was just a kid, I told him about my first two jobs—one in Phoenix and one in Boise, but ultimately I wanted to come back here. I told him how I've been here with Christian the past four years.

I showed him my cake and he ooed and awed, but I did as Royce suggested and let him taste a slice. He photographed the cake, the slice, the cake with the missing slice, and me next to all three.

"This is delicious, Blake. And beautiful." He picked up one of my cherry blossoms. "I would have thought they were real," he shook his head, then took a bite of the little sugar flower.

"That's the idea." I grinned, my cheeks hurting from our talk and all the smiling.

"So, why the *Cherry Blossom Festival*? Tell me what that means to you."

I wasn't exactly sure what he meant. "I mean, it's a city favorite. It celebrates the Japanese culture, but it's more than that too. It celebrates our differences and makes those things that are special even more so." I breathed out, going over my words mentally—did they make any sense? His question tripped me up a little. "I mean, *that*, and they asked me." I laughed a little, nervous energy rising inside of me again.

"Wait, you didn't seek them out?"

I knit my brows. "No. No, they found me."

"Huh," he said, sounding confused. He flipped through his notes. "Fran—ah, Fran Tanaka said that making this cake was your idea or maybe—" He paused, flipping through more notes.

I sat on the edge of my stool. "I—I don't know who that is. Yes, the design is my idea, but it's a job. They came to me. Royce Valentine works for the festival and he hired me."

Cameron scratched his head, still flipping through pages. "Right." He smiled, stopping on one page and tapping at the scribble in his notebook. "Royce Valentine. The guy who called me about the interview. He hired you, then?"

"Yes, he did," I said, on the defense.

His eyes scanned back to his notes. "Right, okay. My bad."

My pounding heart slowed. That's right—*I'm* right. But about what exactly?

"Fran said, their web designer, Roy—that must be Royce," he glanced up, "decided to donate the cake." He held out a hand. "I assumed you were in on that donation."

"Donate?" Heat blossomed in my cheeks. "No, this is a regular ol' job." A legit job—a *big* job. Where did he come up with the word donation? "Royce is helping the committee with different items this year. This was one of those things." I pulled my hair back at my nape, wringing it into a twist, and then letting go.

He pointed at his notes. "Fran said you are not an *official* vendor. She said this is a donation, they chose to accept, because of their relationship with Mr. Valentine." He swallowed, his words slowing. "She gave me a list of the vendors. You aren't on it. She specifically said this was Mr. Valentine's idea, not hers."

My mouth went dry—I don't think I could have swallowed. I stood, held up both my tremoring hands, then crossed my arms. "I —who is this Fran woman, anyway?"

"She's the president of the *Cherry Blossom Festival* committee. She's the one in charge." He shook his head. "I assumed you knew her. But then, I guess it's Mr. Valentine who's hired you."

I paced, my bare feet padding along the cold hard tile floor. "But why—" I shook my head. "Why would he tell me that the festival wanted me? He said they loved my design, my flavors, he said they would do just about anything to have me make this cake." I shrugged, a delirious laugh crying from my mouth. "Why—why would he say that?"

Cameron's face had gone pale. "I... don't... know." He stood and began gathering his things.

"But they—they paid me."

"Mr. Valentine paid you." He tucked his pen into his messenger bag and cleared his throat. "I think I have everything I need. Thanks for the interview, Blake." He nodded, seeming to feel sorry for me—and yet I wasn't exactly sure why—I wasn't sure what had just happened. "The cake is excellent. The best I've eaten." He paused, then set a scrap of notebook paper on the counter before walking to the door, unlocking it himself, and slipping outside.

"I don't understand what just happened." The blood had drained from my face and I rocked on my feet, a little lightheaded. What happened? Why would Royce hire me? Why would he lie to me?

I peered down at the paper Cameron had left.

Fran Tanaka- 303-555-3829

Without thought for my health or sanity or for what I might say, I dialed the number. Chances are she wouldn't even answer—

"This is Fran."

My mouth moved without any words and then quickly, I produced, "Ms. Tanaka?"

"Yes?"

"This is Blake Minola with *Much Ado About Cakes*."

She paused. "Umm—"

She doesn't even know my name. Heat flashed over my chilled body—totally humiliated.

Then finally, she said, "Roy's baker?"

"Yeah," I slumped onto a stool, my head in my hands. "Um, I'm sorry to bother you, but can you tell me how I was hired to bake this cake for the *Cherry Festival?*"

"As far as we're concerned, you weren't. This is a donation."

A lump formed in my throat. "A donation?"

"Yes, I mean no offense, Ms. Minola. We've had our vendors planned for almost a year now. Roy vouched for you. He practically begged for you. And your cake was good."

Good? I could cry with the average word.

"But our vendor signs have been made. Our lineup is created. I told Roy we'd find a spot for your donation. That's the best I can do." She wasn't horrid—not really, just down to business. Just downright honest.

My voice shook. "Can—can you tell me *why?* Why did he care about including me, about this cake?"

Fran's chuckle rang through—short and loud. "I thought you'd know. A friend trying to help a friend? He never said."

My turn to laugh—hearty and sour. Royce didn't even like me when he walked into this shop asking me to bake a cake. So why? Why did he do it?

"I take it you don't know. But you did believe that I'd hired you?"

I nodded—though she couldn't see me.

A tap on the window, just outside, brought my gaze up from the counter.

Royce.

CHAPTER THIRTY-TWO

Royce

I raised my brows, anxious to hear about Blake's interview. With her cell at her ear, she stared at me, her face blank—and a little pale.

Tilting my head, I mouth, *Is everything okay?*

She dropped her hand—phone in its clutches—to her side. She glanced at the thing for only a second before hitting the end button and tossing it with a loud clang onto the metal counter.

"Blake?" I said, moving toward her, but she held up a hand—a stop sign, and I halted in my tracks, confused.

"Who hired me to make this cake?"

The blood drained from my face. I could feel it as it ran out of my head and into my toes. Fear washed over me. My mouth moved, I spoke, but the words didn't feel like mine—because *I* wouldn't lie to her. "The...*Cherry Festival.*"

Her brows knit and she refused to look away from me. "Fran?"

Unblinking, I swallowed down the lump forming in my throat. "Y—es." The word came out long and slow and full of dishonesty.

"Why are you lying?" She spat, but she held her hands to her chest as if she were hurting. "I know, Royce. I know she didn't. I know the festival rejected your request for my cake. What I don't understand is why you even requested it."

My jaw clenched. This wasn't how I wanted this conversation to go—or even begin. "Okay," I breathed out, searching for my confidence. I wasn't ready for it all to end. For us to end. But I couldn't lie again, either. My confidence disappeared, I'd have to suffice by telling her with cowardice. "Juliana was worried about you."

"My sister?" Her eyes went wide and she plopped onto the stool she stood next to. "You knew my sister before—"

"No," I shook my head with vigor. "I promise. I didn't. She knows my cousin."

"Jack."

I nodded. "Yeah, Jack. She just wanted you to have a project that made you happy. No more gender reveals. Jack thought I could help." I licked my lips, talking faster and faster as I went. "I said I would." I gulped, knowing I needed to tell her the whole truth—not part, but all. "And if my efforts paid off then Jack would recommend me for a promotion at work."

She breathed out a coughing, crying, hysterical laugh. "You lied to me to get ahead in your job?" Blinking, she brought her eyes from the counter back to my face.

I swallowed. I stared. I couldn't answer.

Then, as if knowing I left something out—something that I wanted to tell, but that my heart and mouth struggled to get out, she asked, "Why did you ask me out? Why did you flirt with me?" She ran a hand down her face. "I'm so stupid," she muttered to herself.

"You're not." I shook my head, wishing I could sit next to her. If I could touch her, maybe I could fix this. "But—"

Another hysterical laugh, "But?"

"But Jack and I," I shut my eyes, "mostly me, I thought, after meeting you... After," I cleared my throat, "after seeing your reaction to Neal that maybe you needed more than a win in just your career."

"No—*no*. You kept asking me out. You kept flirting—all because..." Her breathing went haggard. "All because I'm some pathetic loser? What was your plan? You were going to shackle yourself to my side, for life, all for the sake of a job? That seems like a pretty big sacrifice, Royce." She held her chest and huffed. I feared she'd hyperventilate or have some kind of attack.

"I planned to date you for a while... and then you'd break up with me." My mouth had gone dry with the words that might as well have dug my own grave.

She'd peered at me, angry and sad, and questioning all at once.

"I had hoped to build your confidence." My jaw clenched and I ground my teeth with the confession. "You'd break up with me and have the upper hand."

"This is crazy." She shook her head, her hands pressed to her temples.

I couldn't help it, I rushed to the counter and crouched to meet her eye to eye. "Blake, I couldn't do it, though. I didn't want you to break up with me. I fell for you and I want this. I want us."

"Us?" She hitched her head backward, looking at me. "*This*," she said, pointing from me to her, "is fictional! You made it up!"

"No," I snatched up her hand, holding it to my chest. "This is real." Tears formed in my eyes, but I didn't care. I blinked them away, letting them run.

"This is real?" she said, her own tears forming.

I nodded, bringing her fingers to my lips.

"Then, I guess your plan worked, Royce. I'm breaking up with you." A sob fell from her chest. "Look at me," she said, false joy in her tone and a forced, sad smile on her lips. "I've got the upper hand for once."

She stood, no shoes on her feet, then as if her knees buckled, she slumped down. I lunged, catching her before she could hit the

189

ground. Blake turned her head into my chest, refusing to look at me, but not strong enough to stand on her own. Her tears soaked through my shirt, drowning my bare skin.

She stilled, like dead weight in my hands and I didn't know what to do with her. I had done this. I had broken Blake—*again*. Again, she'd been hurt. But this time because of me.

Gaining some strength, she pushed away from me. She sat back onto the stool, her head in her hands.

"Blake," I cried, willing her to look at me.

Her eyes stayed glued to the counter, never gracing my face. "The worst thing about Neal isn't that he left me, it's that he lied to me. You're both liars."

"What can I do?

"Leave," she said, her wet lashes fluttering as she drew her gaze up to look at me. "Just go."

CHAPTER THIRTY-THREE

Juliana

I laid next to Blake, waiting for her to wake. She'd slept for hours, crying every now and then, even in sleep. Sometime in the night, she woke.

"Jewels?" she said, her voice groggy and weak.

"I'm here." I tightened my arm about her waist, praying she wouldn't push me away. The ache in my throat—like a bubble growing bigger and bigger, burst. I let out a sob and then said, "I'm sorry. I never meant to hurt you. You were so sad, so miserable, all the time. And I just—I wanted my sister back."

She sighed, blowing out a breath, but didn't push me away.

"I should have given you more time," I said, swiping at the moisture on my cheeks.

"It had been more than a year."

I blinked, trying to see her better in the dim room. "You aren't mad at me?"

"I'll get over it."

"Royce," I began but didn't make it far.

"You manipulated a job for me. Don't ever do that again, by the way—but you did it because you love me. Because you worried over me. Royce Valentine kissed me to win a promotion." Her loathing tone said she hated him, but I'd seen her at the shop. I'd heard her cry over him. I knew that hardness to be a thin protective shell, a wall she put up to block out the pain she felt.

"I'm—" I began, unsure if I should say anything. I treaded thinly, myself. "I'm not so sure about that."

She rolled away from me on her bed. "He said as much, Juliana. I'm a fool. *Again.*"

"You were never a fool." I rubbed my hand down her arm and back again.

"I am!" Her back shook with a new bout of tears. "I hate that I'm crying. He isn't even my type. Why did I like him?"

"He was nice to you."

"Fake!" she barked through a wave of cries.

"He believed in your work," I said, knowing it hadn't all been a farce. I'd seen him. I'd talked to him. I'd *threatened* him! He couldn't be all—

"Fake!" she cried again. "He did what he had to do to get me a job. He did what he thought would make me less miserable to win a bet. He did it all to win his promotion."

"Blake," I moaned.

But she wasn't finished. "The only thing real about Royce Valentine occurred when I was drunk and he exposed his conceited colors—at that stupid engagement party."

Rolling over onto my back, I pressed my palms into my eye sockets, but not even that stopped my tears from my spilling. My shoulders shook. I did this to her. I broke my already fragile sister. Blake lay there—worse than ever—and I could only blame myself.

"Why are you crying?" she said and I removed my hands to see her on her other side staring at me. "I'm the one who was humiliated. I'm the one he lied to."

I covered my face again. "And none of it would have happened had I not asked Jack about job opportunities for you."

She pulled my arms down, though I wanted to keep my red, swollen face covered. "You didn't ask him to find me a *man*, did you?"

I couldn't help it. I snorted. "No." Letting out a long breath, I peered over at her. "I'm sorry."

She wrapped one arm around my waist, pinning my arms to my stomach, her head falling to my shoulder. "I'm sorry too. I know I haven't been myself for a long time." She shuddered out another breath. "Why did I like him so much, Jewels? Why?"

"Maybe he wasn't all bad."

She stiffened with my words—but then said, "He showed interest in my work. Neal never did that. Neal didn't even know the name of my shop until recently, when his *wife* brought him in."

The warmth and dampness from her tears seeped through my shirt and onto my shoulder. I wiggled one hand free of her pin and brushed my fingers across her head and down her long dark hair.

"We had fun, but we talked too. I told him about Mom."

I tilted my head to see her wet lashes flutter up. "You did?" Blake didn't talk about Mom.

"Neal didn't want to hear about her. It's hard enough talking about her to someone who cares." She sniffed.

I wrapped my arm more tightly about her. "Yeah. I get that."

"He met dad before—before I even knew I liked him! Neal and I were engaged when he finally agreed to meet Dad."

I smirked. What a funny night—watching Dad interact with Royce. "Do you think Dad liked him?"

"What does it matter? None of it was real."

Still, I wasn't so sure of that. Maybe Royce could have majored in acting—what did I know? But it seemed pretty sincere to me. "He's the reason I came to the shop."

Her breath hitched. Like she skipped one breath with the realization.

193

"He was worried. He was sick over it all. He called Jack, but then just asked for my number and called me. I think he was afraid Jack wouldn't sound as urgent, that he wouldn't get me there quick enough."

She sniffed beside me. "Guilty conscience."

"Maybe. He seemed really worried."

She slid her head from my shoulder and lay on her back, staring up at the ceiling. "Stop taking his side."

"I'm not. I couldn't."

"Then, stop trying to make me forgive him. I can't," her voice cracked, "I can't forgive him, Juliana. I can't."

CHAPTER THIRTY-FOUR

Blake

So, I baked a week early.

I needed to do this.

I needed it done.

I needed to make this cake and give it to Royce. It might be the only thing that would heal the constant ache in my heart. He had hired me to bake a cherry blossom cake. The festival hadn't wanted it—they hadn't wanted me. But I'd still been paid. I'd still sketched and researched and worked my tail off creating two hundred individual and unique confectionary cherry blossoms.

I would make this cake.

Even more so, because I'm certain he believed I wouldn't do it at all.

I was going to finish this cake and leave it on his doorstep.

He can eat the whole dang thing himself.

My amaretto icing mixed and smoothed to perfection—and I had a quarter of my cherry blossoms already carefully placed on the top layer of this tri-level masterpiece when the shop door opened. I glanced up and blinked at the sight before me.

I blinked again—because my eyes had to be playing tricks on me. Her short, fire engine red hair feathered to the side and fluffed in the back. Her heels were as tall as Juliana's and her face resembled a porcelain doll.

"Melanie Kucho?" I said, unable to hide my shock.

"Oh good," she crooned, hand fluttering to her chest. "You remember me."

"I—I do," I said, stammering over the words. I had no idea what she would be doing here. In my shop. Talking to *me.*

"I'm here to place an order," she said, a massive grin on her face. "For a cake."

A cake—that thought hadn't even occurred to me. "Oh," I said, again unable to keep any kind of a poker face. "What kind of cake?"

"My assistant ordered the groom's cake for my daughter's wedding shower." Her eyes went wide. "How do you mess up a simple groom's cake?" She threw her hands in the air.

I shrugged. Though I could think of plenty of ways—too much sugar, too much liquid, not enough baking soda, too much baking soda...

Huffing out a breath, Melanie pulled her phone from the handbag hanging from her arm, as if she were a model in a magazine. "This isn't a circus," she said, holding the phone out to me.

A 3D fondant Elvis, dressed in white and gold sat on top of a confectioner's record player. The cake showcased skills—I liked it really, but I concealed my grin. "Not very sophisticated," I said, offering her a sympathetic grimace.

"Exactly. This isn't a child's birthday party!"

I shoved my hands into my apron pockets. "The combined bride and groom wedding shower, right?"

She smiled, "Yes, Juliana must have told you."

Sure—that and Royce had asked me to be his date a week ago. That wouldn't be happening now.

"Perfect. You already know the event. And..." she said, her gaze roving over my cherry blossom cake creation. "Royce wasn't wrong. You have impeccable skills. What do you say? The shower is tomorrow."

"Wait. Royce? Royce told you to hire me?" My heart plummeted. Would I never be able to get a real job on my own merit?

"Darling, I'm the boss." She smiled sweetly, happy to teach me this lesson. "No one tells me to do anything." She sighed, looking down at her watch. "Royce has been talking about Blake's cakes for two months now. I am here of my own free will." She scanned over my cherry blossom tiers again. "And, I like what I see."

My insides jolted. She liked what she saw. Melanie, of all people, wouldn't have hired me—for a favor. I knew that without a doubt.

I liked time with a project, and she wasn't giving me much. But I knew I could do it. And the way Melanie studied my cherry blossom cake... I *wanted* to do it. I wanted to prove my worth to myself, to Melanie, and to anyone else who wondered if I was the right person for this job.

"I'll do it," I said. "Any requests?"

Her eyes turned to slits, thinking. "Not Elvis."

I laughed and brushed the corn flour from my fingers. "I think I can handle that."

"Here," Melanie said, holding out her hand with a credit card and a sticky note. "The address to the shower. Can you drop it off between five and six? I'd have my assistant come by for it, but she's busy looking for a new job."

Yikes.

I didn't normally handle delivery duty, but I didn't have the energy to argue with her. Besides, the shop wouldn't be opened tomorrow. We took Sundays off. I cleared my throat, attempting

197

not to be intimidated by this woman that Juliana worked with on a regular basis. "Sure. I can do that."

"Fabulous. See you then."

~

*I*t took two more hours for me to finish the cherry blossom cake.

It stood three layers high, pearly white, with a vine of cherry blossoms intricately running down and around each tier like a bridal veil or a waterfall. Perfection, exactly as my mind had envisioned it.

I sat on a stool right in front of my masterpiece, tears pooling in my eyes and slipping down my cheeks. My heart leapt and broke all at once.

He hadn't been by the shop and I'd blocked his number. No texts. No calls. No sightings of Royce Valentine—not in the last two weeks, not since the day he'd made a fool of me and broke my heart.

And now, I planned to walk up to his door and deliver a cake.

He'd turned me into a masochist.

A masochist who missed stolen kisses, rowdy laughter, and tender talks.

"I hate you, Royce Valentine," I said over my sobs. I blinked, looking up to see my boss staring down at me.

Christian tilted his head, looking from me to my cake. He knew bits and pieces of the *Cherry Festival* nightmare.

"Now you're lying to yourself," he said.

I crammed my eyes closed. "I want to hate him."

"I know." He plopped down next to me, his long lanky arms hanging at his sides. "But that cake, Blake. It's incredible."

I sniffed. "Yeah?"

"An edible piece of art." He dug in his pocket, then held up his cell. "Do you mind?" he asked.

I shook my head and watched as Christian snapped a few pictures of my work. "Have you talked to him?"

I said nothing, afraid to talk, afraid to move. I'd only break down again.

"Maybe you should." He waited.

And instead of sitting there half the day, I spoke. "Maybe I shouldn't."

He shrugged and lobbed his oval face to the side, watching me. "You'll have to deliver that beauty," he said.

"You—"

"I can't do it." His lips formed a flat line. "Blake do you know why I hired you four years ago?"

My brows knit with his change in subject. "Uhh, because I applied?"

He smirked. "Sure, that. But in that interview you said with more fervor than I had felt in years—*I love cake*. You said it as if you were a parent talking about your one and only child. Then you showed me your portfolio like they were pictures of your newborn babes."

I flicked my gaze to the ceiling, thinking about that portfolio—some of those pictures I'd be happy to burn at this point. I'd grown. A lot.

He laughed at my reaction. "You aren't wrong—those cakes may have been a bit wanting." He gave me a wry smile. "But you believed in yourself, that was clear. I saw potential in what those cakes could one day be. I saw who you could become." His brows bounced and he tilted his head toward my cherry blossom baby.

The right corner of my mouth tickled with the urge to grin.

"And then you met Neal," Christian's brows knit and his blue eyes drag over to peer at my face, "and some of that spirit died."

I searched the tabletop—no it didn't... Did it? "Is that why I got put on gender reveal duty?"

"No—ahh—" His head rocked from side to side. "Maybe a little." He lifted one shoulder and one hand, in an apologetic shrug.

"I know you don't love them." Christian's arms flapped at his sides. "But you're good at them. And man, they keep us in business."

I snorted. We did seem to get a large amount of gender reveal orders—even with my "mistakes".

"But something changed the last two months. I don't know if it was Royce. Or this cake. But your fire came back." His brows rose and he smiled at me. "With a vengeance." He held a hand out toward my cake. "And look what you made."

"It's pretty great, right?"

"It's better than great." He stood from his seat. "Let me help you get it inside the delivery box. And then, you're going to deliver that cake, because an artist should always be proud of their work."

~

I sat in front of Royce's building, thankful for his first-floor apartment. This cake weighed *a lot*, it had to be at least sixty pounds. My arms burned by the time I lugged it to his door. My heart didn't have time to freak out or melt down with everything inside of me steadying the cake and keeping it off the ground.

Slow and steady, I bent, setting my cake in front of his door, feeling apprehensive about leaving it. How stupid? It was a cake, not a human. But I loved this cake. Christian had said it brought back my fire—but maybe it contained my fire—my spirit.

Before all of my courage could leave me, I set a fist to the door and pounded. A tremor ran through my feet. I wouldn't stay to see his face. This wasn't a gender reveal for Neal Huffmire—someone who never deserved my love. This was like giving half of my heart away to someone that I thought for a second I could have given all of me to.

My chest shuddered with the thought and I turned, my mind tunneling with blackness and sorrow, but I found enough light to see the exit sign.

Before I could reach my car, I heard him. "Blake! Blake!" His huffing breaths grew closer. *"Blakeberry!"* He bellowed, and I stopped.

I turned to face him. He ran his fingers through his dark hair and a waft of cucumber mint assaulted my senses.

"What do you want, Royce?" I said, unable to hide the defeat in my voice.

He blinked, his eyes roving over my face. His hands flapped at his side, smacking against the dark denim of his jeans. His plain gray tee hugged his chest and abs. He looked good, besides the rings beneath his eyes and his disheveled hair. But then, Royce always looked good.

"I miss you," he said, the same defeat from my own tone in his.

I shuffled in place. "So, that's why you haven't called me?"

His forehead wrinkled and he ventured one step off the sidewalk, sharing the blacktop I stood on. "You blocked my number."

Dang. How did he know that? "Stupid Jack," I muttered under my breath.

"Not that I blame you," he said, his forehead furrowed in a row of wrinkles I'd never seen on him before.

"And you've stopped by my apartment or the shop how many times?" I didn't ask to persuade him, I asked to condemn him. He'd played me. He'd played me and I fell for it—hook, line, and sinker.

"I didn't think you'd want to see me."

I nodded my head to the side and muttered to myself once more. "Well, that's accurate."

He leaned my way, as if he wanted to take another step or two closer, but he couldn't. "I never meant to hurt you, Blake."

"No, you never meant to get caught."

"Blake," he moaned, running his hand through his hair again, this time snatching a fist full and holding it there.

With tears close, I opened my car door, slid inside, and started up the engine. I swatted the first one away, but not quick enough to avoid Royce seeing the dumb thing.

With both fists on his head, I watched him mouth my name, before speeding away.

CHAPTER THIRTY-FIVE

Jack

I'd never seen Royce so miserable. I listened as he told me about Blake dropping the cake off on his doorstep—while eating the best cake I'd ever placed in my mouth.

The colossal confectionary tower sat on the table in Royce's kitchen, two slices missing from its top tier.

Royce had hardly touched his slice. "I didn't want to eat it," he said, poking at his slice and staring up at the massive cake in front of us. "But I didn't know what else to do with it. The festival isn't for a week."

"What will you tell Fran?"

He shrugged. "I don't think she'll care. She was never invested like she should have been." He stabbed at his slice. "I failed her on so many levels, Jack."

I knew he wasn't talking about Fran. And I couldn't help but feel responsible. "I shouldn't have asked you to help me. I—"

"Starting a relationship with Blake wasn't your idea. I think she may have gotten over the cake fiasco." He thought a minute. "Maybe not. I don't know."

I didn't know either. I didn't know Blake as well as Royce or Juliana. But I had heard about her plenty from both of them.

"What are you going to do now?"

He lifted one shoulder in a shrug. "She thinks I'm a liar. She doesn't even think she knows the real me."

"Maybe you shouldn't give up." I'd never known Royce to give up on anything. Why was this any different?

His eyes flicked up from his cake to me. "Maybe I should give her some peace. She doesn't want me. And how can I blame her?"

I clenched my jaw. I didn't know how to answer that. I didn't know how to help. "You coming to the party tonight?" I said, instead.

"The wedding shower?" He cringed with the idea.

"Yeah. You should come. It would mean a lot to Charlotte." I stood having finished off my slice. "Mom's got duties for me—I should go."

He nodded. "Yeah. I'm sure I'll show up for a minute. For Charlotte."

I slid the rest of the top tier of Royce's cherry blossom cake onto a plate, knowing he wouldn't care if I took it. He had to get rid of the massive thing somehow. I started for his door, clutching the plate of cake with one hand, but turned around. "Hey, Royce."

"Yeah?"

"I recommended you for the manager position." I licked a spot of icing from my finger. "And not because you fulfilled any bargain. I did it because you deserve it. You've worked hard. You're the best designer I know. And you should have it."

He studied me, his brows knit, not even the semblance of a smile on his lips.

On autopilot, I drove to *The Creative Drive*. Only a few designers ever bothered coming in on Sundays. Still, I might as well leave the cake. I walked it up to our opened work room, down the hall, past the recording and conference rooms, and into the small lobby where so many employees ate their lunch. I set the half-eaten tier in the refrigerator and wrote a quick note, inviting all to eat, then taped it to the fridge door.

The quiet of the office reminded me I had work to do—*actual* work, before Mom used me for slave labor. It wasn't that she couldn't afford to hire men, in fact, she did hire workers, plenty of them. But Mom liked things in a very specific way and she knew that I knew her way.

I stopped in the recording room—remembering that with Royce's interruption I would need to completely restart Juliana's screencast guide of her site.

I clicked open the one I'd made and watched for a minute—then a few longer. I thought maybe I could piece a few things together. But soon realized, I'd recorded my entire conversation with Royce.

My chest pounded—remembering that conversation.

Then—I didn't think. I just clicked.

Opening, my email I sent the video to Juliana. Heart thumping, as if I were doing something wrong or sneaky—though I knew I wasn't—I sent her a quick text.

Email. Now. Show Blake.

CHAPTER THIRTY-SIX

Juliana

$\mathcal{I}$ slammed my laptop closed and pulled the earbuds from my ears. Blinking, I peered at Amy Allen—country music superstar—flipping through my sketches.

A shaky breath left my chest as I glanced at the clock. My appointment with Amy had only begun.

"Everything okay?" she asked, knowing I had excused myself for a minute.

"Yeah," came my instant, non-thinking response. "Um, I—" My heart pattered. "I need to go."

"Go?" She peered up from the current sketch in her hands.

"Yes," I said, feeling more confident in my answer. I loved my job. I was designing Amy Allen's *People* magazine photo op—how could I not? But I loved my sister more. "Yes," I repeated. "I have to. Something's come up and it can't wait." I stood. "You hold on to the sketches. I'll be in touch. Soon."

"What about the fabric swatches?" she said, holding up my catalog of fabrics, a scowl on her normally pretty face.

"Um, you can hold on to those as well." I gathered my computer bag and started for the door.

"Juliana," she said, her tone scolding. "Hold up."

I paused in the doorway. "Ms. Allen, I'm sorry to do this to you. I know your time is valuable. But my sister needs me. I can't fail her now. Even if that means you'd like to replace me with a different designer." I took one step then paused. "If you can be patient with me, I promise it'll be worth it. But I understand if you can't wait." With that, I left. I sped off toward the shop, where I knew Blake would be putting the finishing touches on Eric's groom cake.

~

"Jewels, hey." Flour dusted Blake's cheeks. "Come look at this, will you?"

She didn't even ask why I'd come. For the first time in days, she didn't look completely miserable. It had to be the project Melanie had her working on. Something creative and yummy always cheered Blake.

"It's a dark chocolate cake with fresh strawberries between the layers and a white ganache. I'm going to drip this," she held up a container of melted chocolate down the sides." She bit her cheek, examining her own design. "And I'm thinking tuxedo dipped strawberries for on top."

I glanced at the smooth edges of the frosted, two-tiered cake. The classy design would match Melanie's black and white theme.

"I could place strawberries around the bottom edge, too." She tapped her chin. "Yeah, I think I will." She glanced at me. "Jewels?"

"It's perfect, Blake." I nodded but didn't really think about what I said. "Really great."

"What's with you? You barely looked at it."

I pulled in a breath, my chest expanding until I thought it might burst. Letting out the air with a tremble, I said, "I need to show you something."

"What?" Her eyes returned to her cake. She lifted the tub of melted chocolate, ready to begin her drip, but I placed my hand over her wrist, stopping her.

"You're gonna want to put that down."

Finally, she sat on a stool, staring at my computer screen. "What is this?"

"It's a screencast that Jack made for me. It's to show me around my own website, show me what all the buttons and links can do."

Her brows rose and she slid her gaze back to the waiting groom's cake.

"Please, Blake."

She sighed—a bit over dramatic, and settled her hands in her lap. "Fine. Okay. Shoot!"

I clicked play on the screen and a video of my website came into view. Jack's voice could be heard, but no picture of him showed on the screen.

"Hey Jewels," he said through the computer. "So, I changed the URL name. Design by Juliana is cute. I love it actually, but when people want to find you, they'll just type in your name. So, your new URL is just Juliana Minola."

Blake huffed out a breath and darted a glance my way—a silent: *Really? Why am I watching this? I have actual work to do!*

I pressed a finger to my lips, hushing her, though she hadn't spoken.

"Here you'll see—" Jack said, but then paused.

We could hear a slam in the background and then Royce was speaking. "I have to tell her," he said.

Blake gasped, a hand slapping over her mouth, she blinked from me, then back to the computer.

"Tell... who? What?" Jack said.

"Blake," Royce seemed to growl at his cousin. "What are you doing?"

"Just a screencast for Juliana's new website," Jack said.

We heard a huff, then Royce asked. "Things are going... well?"

"Very," Jack answered.

Their talking paused, fifteen, twenty seconds... though it felt much longer. "I gotta tell her, Jack. The truth." Royce sounded distraught.

"Ahh—I've never been one to condone lying, but... are you sure that's a good idea?" I could just imagine Jack's face as he spoke. His blue-green eyes would be wide, his stare long.

"No," Royce seemed to bark at him, but I couldn't picture his face. No instead, I watched my sisters. Her fingers still pressed to her lips.

Royce continued, "I'm not sure of anything anymore. It's just lying to her—I mean, I'm not. Everything has been so *real*. Yet there's this thing... hanging over my head. And, I don't think I can live with that. She has to know the truth."

"So... tell her," Jack's words were gentle but so unsure. I knew he wanted to help his cousin, to help my sister. But at this point— he'd told me even now, he didn't know how.

My eyes stayed glued to Blake—knowing what came next. "People who fall in love are gluttons for punishment," Royce said, somehow his tone sad and angry all at once. "Were this any other guy, I'd tell him to keep quiet. Why get in trouble over nothing? So, why do I feel compelled to be truthful with her? Why can't I just leave it alone and enjoy what we have?"

"Well," Jack said, "It sounds like you love her."

After a short pause, Royce growled, "It's been two months since we met, Jack."

"Yep."

A sigh—I assumed from Royce. "When did I turn into a glutton?"

Another short pause, my heart beat as I watched Blake, then, Jack said, "So you admit that you love Blake?"

"I admit that I'm a glutton," Royce retorted, clearly upset. "This isn't going to end well."

"You don't know that," Jack said.

"I do." I couldn't see Royce, but my head painted the picture for me—and my heart ached for him, just as it ached for Blake. "I know Blake. She won't forgive me. I wouldn't forgive me."

"But you're still going to tell her?" Jack asked.

Blake stiffened and seemed to hold her breath, waiting for Royce's answer given all those weeks ago. "I am," he said. "I have to. She means too much. She deserves to know."

"When? Will you at least wait until after the festival?"

"I don't know."

"What changes if you wait?"

Quick to answer, Royce said, "Three more weeks of fueled hatred?"

"You're so sure she'll hate you. Maybe she'll thank you for believing in her, for giving her a chance to make something so beautiful." A tear slid down Blake's cheek with Jack's words.

"I don't think she'll see it that way."

"But you don't know."

I paused the video. "That's pretty much it." I sat beside her, resting a hand on her shoulder. "I thought you'd want to know."

She didn't say anything, but another tear fell.

"Blake," I spoke soft, but felt an urgent pull, "was I right to show it to you?"

She nodded, more tears spilling over.

"Does it change anything?" I dipped my head, meeting her eyes. I believed in my heart that it should change things.

She peered up at me, her eyes a puddle of tears, pulling her hands from her puckering lips, she shrugged.

"It has to," I said. "He was going to tell you. He—he loves you, Blake." I set my hands to her cheeks, looking at her and forcing her to look back at me. "He made you happy. And you made him a better person. It's okay to forgive."

"I don't know if I have it in me to try again, Jewels. It hurts so much."

"It only hurts because the loss was so great. Think of all you could gain?"

CHAPTER THIRTY-SEVEN

Royce

I had given cake to every non-allergic, gluten-eating human on my floor, and I still had half a tier. I only wished I'd had business cards to pass out as well. If they never mentioned my name, Blake would be getting new customers, all from my building. If they made the mistake and told her I sent them, she would likely turn them out without another word.

I stared at the half of a tier still sitting on my counter. Every inch of it made me think of Blake. I ran my hands down my face. I couldn't sit here any longer. I couldn't stare at this cake thinking about how Blake would never forgive me for what I'd done. I'd go mad.

I snagged my suit, still in its dry cleaning bag, and headed out the door. I was supposed to arrive, like any other guest attending Charlotte and Eric's wedding shower, at six. So what? I'd only be three hours early. I could help set up. I knew Jack would already be there—being the dutiful son—and he'd put me to work.

I'd never been inside the historical Shakespeare Club before, but I wasn't surprised when Aunt Melanie chose to rent a venue for a *shower* where most people held the actual wedding. By the time Melanie was finished with this wedding, Charlotte would feel as though she'd been married three times already.

I could hear the men out back, so I headed straight there, instead of going inside the big stone building. The massive yard had green hedges outlining the separate villas. Gray stones made up walkways and a large rectangular floor at the center of the yard. Workers set up tables around the stone floor. A single table had been placed in the center of the floor with space around it for— whatever Aunt Melanie had planned.

I scanned the grounds for Jack and found him giving a man, holding a cart of chairs, directions. I tossed my suit, in its protective casing, onto a nearby hedge and made my way over to my cousin.

"I know what the manager told you," Jack was saying, "but Melanie would like every chair covered thirty minutes prior to guests arriving."

The worker clenched his jaw, his chin to his chest, and stared at my cousin.

"I understand it would be easier to do it now. Ms. Kucho would rather the elements not have a chance to muss the coverings in the meantime."

Silent, the man huffed out a breath and wheeled his cart away.

"How is it you always end up on duty at these things?"

Jack shrugged, seeming not to care. "It's Charlotte's big day—"

"One of the many," I said under my breath.

"And I am the only son. So—"

"Right. Well, I'm here to help."

"Really?" he said, brows raised with surprise—but relief.

"Really."

Jack clapped his hands. No false pretenses claiming he didn't need me. Good ol' Jack. "There are dozens of floral arrangements in the building. The florist set them up in there and left. The party is outdoors." He shook his head—just what he needed, one more thing to do today.

"Right, no problem. Any place, in particular, I should place them?"

"If you get them out here, in this villa, Matthieu will direct someone where they should go."

"I can do that," I said.

Inside the Shakespeare club was a massive room, large baskets, and vases filled with white flowers of all different varieties, many with black stripes or dots through pearly white petals. When Aunt Mel had a theme, she didn't venture from it.

I had just lobbed up my first basket of flowers when Melanie came inside through the front entrance.

"Royce! Wait for me, dear," she called, waving a hand my way while turning to talk to a girl with a clipboard.

I adjusted the weighty basket in my hands and waited for my aunt to approach.

"You came to help Jack. You angel."

I smiled and leaned down, so she could kiss my cheek hello.

"What are you doing with that?" she asked.

"Oh, the florist set them all up in here, I'm taking them outside."

She squinted, grinning at me—like she had since I was a boy. "And you aren't afraid to get your hands dirty."

"Nope." Though my arms would fall off if I didn't change positions soon. This basket had to weigh eighty pounds. "I'm just gonna take this—"

"Royce," she said again. "This isn't a time or place for business, but you know me. I don't appreciate laziness or time wasting. And..." she seemed to study me, "yes, let's move forward."

The massive basket drooped in my arms. I didn't follow her train of thought, but I'd worked with Melanie long enough to know when a conversation was going to take some time and some deciphering. I set the basket on the ground at our feet, knowing that meant I'd have to heft it up again. Standing straight, I huffed out a breath. "Move forward?"

"Yes, Jack believes that you—*not him*—are the right man for the floor manager job. You've always done good work, Royce. But more importantly, you are a team player. I think my son is right. You are the person who will lead our floor with an example of quality and effort." She nodded.

Just like that. One small declaration. One little nod. And the job was mine. *Mine.* I'd been aspiring to this job for years and without any type of warning, Melanie was leaving it right in my lap.

I pulled in a breath—waiting for the elation to come. This is what I wanted. This is what I worked for. So... why did it feel so erroneous?

"You have no words?" she said, her white teeth gleaming with her grin.

"I... I... don't know what to say." I pushed the rim of my glasses up.

Aunt Melanie laughed. "All you have to say is, *I accept.*"

I forced out a breathy chuckle.

"Royce?" she said, seeing through my false laughter.

"I—" I crammed my eyes shut and shook my head. "I've wanted this a long time."

Her face lit with her nod.

"And yet, I cannot accept."

Her forehead wrinkled, her brows high on her head. "You *cannot?*"

This job would always be tainted with what I did to Blake. It would be a reminder for the rest of my life that she couldn't forgive me, that I'd lost her. "I cannot," I said, my insides feeling stronger with the words. For the first time in weeks, I didn't feel like my heart might shrivel up and die. I'd made the right decision. This job would never make me happy. Not like I thought it would. Not anymore. "Aunt Mel, I love you. You are an incredible woman.

You've paved a way for me, for Jack, as well as for women in the industry everywhere. I will forever be grateful."

Her wrinkles smoothed away, but her eyes stayed wide and questioning with my compliments.

"And—" I nodded, strengthened by something inside of me that said—*this is right,* "I quit. Err—I'm giving my two weeks' notice."

"Royce!" she squawked, one hand on her slender hip.

I kissed her cheek, as she had mine moments before, and bent to retrieve my stupidly heavy basket of flowers. "I've got work to do," I said. "I'll see you tonight."

CHAPTER THIRTY-EIGHT

Blake

"Is this necessary?" I asked more on instinct than anything. I had after all, for the first time in either of our lives, asked Juliana to come by, to dress and doll me up.

Her black skirt flowed around her as she sat me down for make-up and hair first. She outlined my lips in a mulberry reddish purple, a color I had never even considered wearing before she pulled it from her Mary Poppins bag.

"Oh shush," she said, eyes still on my mouth.

"Why are there two garment bags?" I asked, with her lift of the liner. "You're already dressed."

"I'm giving you options."

I raise my recently penciled brows. "That's never happened before."

"Yeah, well I almost brought a red dress, but I don't think Melanie would have let you in the door. She likes her themes. Still, you would have stood out fantastically." She looked off into space, dreamy-eyed for a second.

"So, what did you bring?" I slid my gaze to the garment bags.

"Patience," she said, as she filled in the rest of my lips. "You do not utilize your lips like you should."

I cinched my brows and breathed out a laugh. "What does that mean?"

"You have the best lips. They bow perfectly and they're so full."

"So?"

"So, you never accentuate with gloss or liner."

"I wear balm every single day," I said.

Juliana sighed. "Chap-stick doesn't count." She dabbed my lips once more. "There. You're done. All right. Let's talk clothes."

"We're going to be late at this rate," I said, looking at the clock.

"No, Cinderella. *You're* going to be late. I'm going to be right on time."

"But—my cake. It wouldn't be professional for me to come in late," I stammered.

Juliana's long dark lashes flicked to the top of her brows, her eyes rolling up to the ceiling for a second. "I will take your cake, so that it's on time. You may come a quarter past six."

I wasn't sure about this. My insides were a mess. "Why?" I whined.

"Because, you'll make an entrance, everyone else will already be there. And I want to see Royce's face when you walk in."

"I don't know Jewels. I—"

"If things were different, you'd *feel* differently. Well, guess what? Things *are* different, Blake. You heard that video, just as I did. He made mistakes. But then, haven't we all?"

I swallowed—more excuses leaving my lips. "What if they won't let me in?"

"Your name will be on the guest list since you're supposed to be bringing the cake. You'll be fine." She set a hand on my shoulder. "I'd hug you, but I don't want to mess up my masterpiece." Then standing, she pointed at the bags on my bed. "I don't care which

218

you choose, but you're wearing those shoes," she said, nodding toward the shoe box on the floor next to us.

I flipped open the box lid. Strappy red shoes, with a five-inch heel lay inside. "Red?" I said, but really my eyes stayed glued to those heels.

"You have to stand out," she said. "A red dress may get you kicked out, but red shoes will only get you envied." She waved, her fingers nodding at me, indicating that she would be leaving. With *my* cake.

My heart beat faster. "Fine," I called out as she walked away, "but if I break my ankle—" Before I could finish, she'd shut the door.

I opened bag number one, feeling odd, as if I were on an episode of the dating game, and pulled out a sleeveless, vintage dress. The solid black top had an A-line neck. It attached to a flaring white skirt that would hit at my knee, floral silhouettes sprinkles across the soft, pearly material. A ribbon with a bow tied around the middle—one neat little package.

I smiled at the little cocktail dress. "Okay, bachelor number two," I said, picking up the second bag, and unzipping it.

The minute I pulled the jumpsuit from the bag, I started giggling. The soft black silk ran the full length of my body, spilling over my hands like an ebony waterfall. A sleek white collar—resembling more a scarf, covered one shoulder and ran down the length of one arm. I loved the elegant minimalism of the suit and knew in an instant it would be my choice. The red shoes would just peek out beneath the length of the flowing pant legs, and I even liked the idea of that.

I breathed out a shaky breath and began to undress.

My phone buzzed to life and I paused, looking down at the numbers stringing across my screen. On any other day, I would have ignored it. So, today of all days—when I didn't have time for it—of course, I felt the need to answer.

"Hello?"

"Blake Minola?" A faintly familiar voice asked.

"Yes?"

"This is Fran Tanaka, from the *Cherry Blossom Festival.*"

"Oh," I sat, in just my undergarments, Juliana's outfits on either side of me. I crossed my newly shaven legs, my palm suddenly feeling sweaty. "Hi."

"Hi," she returned. "Uh, I'm wondering if you can help me."

"Me?"

"Well, yes. My dessert vendor backed out on me last minute." She sighed. "You can imagine my disappointment when I contacted Royce Valentine about the cake you were supposed to be making."

My heart thudded—almost in defense. I had given that cake to Royce a week early. It would not be in eating shape come June 25th. "Oh." I clamped down on my freshly glossed lip.

"Yes, I was not happy at all when he told me that he'd *eaten* his donation." She sounded as if she could kill him and a week ago— heck twenty-four hours ago that may have made me laugh. But today—I could only think that it wasn't *all* his fault. When I said nothing, Fran went on. "An entire cake!"

"It wouldn't have been good by the time the festival came," I said, but defending him came slowly. My wounded heart struggled to say anything. I was still trying to figure out how to heal—even with this new information Juliana had brought me. She'd talked me into going to this party, but what was I supposed to say or do when I saw Royce?

"Yes, well poor planning on Royce's part." She sighed again and I opened my mouth, but I couldn't speak quick enough. I didn't have time to claim my guilt. "So, I'm wondering, Ms. Minola, would you still be willing to make something for the festival? Not a tiered complete cake though. A finger food. Something we don't need to provide utensils for. A cupcake of sorts?"

My head spun. The festival wanted me after all?

"I was impressed with your work, I just didn't have room." She cleared her throat. "At the time. I do now."

I'd used all my sugar blossoms on Royce's cake. Did I even have time to make more? I honestly wasn't sure at that second. But I'd figure it out later. "I'll do it," I said.

~

*C*ooled by the fresh summer breeze, I followed the signs from the front of the Shakespearean Club to a backyard that was more like an enormous garden. Goosebumps rose on my one bare arm. By some miracle, I walked in Juliana's red shoes like I'd been wearing them all my life. I followed the stone walkway to where a dozen round tables staggered around a center area, almost a stone dance floor. In the middle sat a table with a white bride's cake and my dark contrasting groom's cake.

I ignored the turning heads around me—they all mixed into one, in their black and white—and studied my cake. I liked it. I was proud of my work and I needed to start behaving that way—rather than shocked when someone praised me.

The crowd started to sit—just as Juliana said they would—and my nerves went from moderately jumbled to ready to hyper-ventilate.

Juliana had said—just come. Just see what happens. *Maybe* talk to Royce.

But could I do that? I didn't know what to say—even after hearing his remorse and confession on that video. My heart pattered in my chest, so much that I wondered if everyone could see it. Did I stand out amongst the sea of black and white? If I did, I didn't think my clothes were the cause, but rather my nerves —blaring.

I hadn't even found my sister.

I roved over the cluster of people, searching for Juliana in her black and white cocktail dress. But instead, I found *him*. Royce

221

stood across the yard, his eyes on me. He didn't smile, but he didn't frown either. In his dark suit and long thin tie, I was reminded once again of James Bond. 007, watching me...

I blinked, my brain telling my eyes to turn away, yet struggling to do so.

"Friends," Melanie Kucho's voice sang out, loud and clear amongst the chatter, "please take your seats."

The tables circled the floor in one large O. I stood next to one and like an obedient dog, I sat on Melanie's command.

Royce took three steps—starting for the center of the stone floor, coming to me—when Melanie set a hand on his arm. This time I couldn't hear her, but I saw her business-like face, and her hands shoo him to the closest table.

Still, his eyes bore into me and my heart stung with its rapid beat. Why did I let Juliana talk me into this? What was I supposed to do now? Talk to Royce? I couldn't talk to Royce. I couldn't be here. I breathed, in through my nose, out through my mouth.

And yet, I was here. I'd come to Melanie's party, in some fancy jumpsuit to boot. In fact, I'd *driven* myself here. I hadn't been forced. And in truth, I did have something to say.

Just like that, as quickly as my grieving head clouded, it cleared.

I blew out, my breath shaky, but strong.

I did have something to say—and I wouldn't leave without saying it.

CHAPTER THIRTY-NINE

Royce

*B*lake sat clear across the villa.

Blake? Here? My hope soared—could it be for me? Why else would she be here?

And then I could hear her—calling me cocky and egotistical.

She might be right.

But I didn't care. I wanted to believe she'd come for me. The goddess, across the room, had come to see *me*.

"We'll toast," Aunt Melanie said to the crowd, interrupting my thoughts. "And we'll drink." She grinned, holding up her glass, already filled with champaign, and a peal of humming laughter spread throughout the guests. "And we'll dance."

The crowd clapped, except for me, I couldn't stop staring at Blake, Melanie's words an afterthought in my brain.

"So, let's toast this happy couple. Yeah?" Melanie peered about as if looking for someone to share their thoughts. But I knew my aunt. She always had a plan. "Our maid of—"

"I'll make a toast!" Blake shouted from across the way. She stood, her dark hair falling onto the white top of her jumpsuit.

A hushed silence fell and for the first time, I gave Aunt Melanie my full attention—just like everyone else in the room.

Hailey, Charlotte's maid of honor, slumped in her seat, irritated —Aunt Mel had been about to call on her.

Blake's gaze stayed glued to my aunt, waiting for confirmation.

"Ah," Aunt Melanie smiled, false, but sure, "Of course, dear." She held out her hand and smoothly lowered herself into her seat next to Charlotte.

"Who is that?" I heard Charlotte whisper.

"That's our baker."

I ran my fingers through my hair, nervous for Blake. This wasn't like her. She liked to stay in the back laughing and joking. I could see her quietly heckling someone toasting—but deliver one herself... *no*. And here? Never.

My hands twitched.

"Hello," she said, her tone clear but scratchy.

I sat on the edge of my chair, not wanting to miss one syllable.

"I—I wanted to wish you well," she said, but it was clear she didn't know where the bride and groom sat. Her eyes scanned the group, blinking fiercely when they reached my corner of the rockery.

Just to my left, a moan of nerves ground out. I glanced to see Juliana, her eyes boring into her sister, her fist pressed to her lips.

"I need to voice something I've learned about hearts," Blake said, snatching back my full attention. She brushed one of the big curls at her cheek behind one ear. "See, people will let you down. Again and again." She sniffed and finally her gaze stopped on me— it didn't just pass by. It said—YOU let me down.

My pulse quickened and I pulled at my collar, too warm for my shirt and jacket.

"They'll cheat, and lie, and pretend. You'll tell yourself to just trust your instincts. And that isn't bad advice—until you can't anymore. Because eventually, your heart will get involved—not just your instincts. And sometimes your heart will take you down a path you never should have gone."

She watched me now, not even disguising that her gaze, these words, this moment was for me. And I listened, she deserved that at the very least, even if I shattered inside with each word.

"No," she pressed her rosy lips together, "hearts cannot be trusted."

"Mother," I heard Charlotte's whispering moan.

I reached out a hand—instinctively—holding Melanie back. "Let her finish."

"Hearts are easily deceived. A heart will never see the betrayal coming." Her chest heaved, but she didn't cry. She held a hand to her chest, licked her lips, and went on, "And then, even after when your stupid heart is shattered, it will try to convince you that he didn't mean it. He didn't want to hurt you." She crammed her eyes closed for a second. "Hearts will tell you that you can still be together. A heart will attempt to turn hate into love—even," a shuddering breath fell from her rosy lips, "even when it shouldn't." She shook her head and I tried to make sense of the glisten on her cheeks... a tear? "I don't want to love him," she cried. "Because love is too fragile and my heart," she blew out a breath, struggling to keep her composure, "my heart isn't strong enough. Not anymore."

A deafening silence fell as she ended her speech. A small whimper sounded from my cousin. Beside Charlotte, Jack stood. He raised his glass. "To love," he said, peering out at the crowd and, in true Jack fashion, attempting to make things right for everyone. "Blake's right. That which brings us the greatest joy also has the ability to bring us the greatest sorrow. So, Charlotte, Eric, love each other sweetly, honestly, and with all you have. Be happy, little sister."

"Here, here!" Melanie crowed and the throng raised their glasses in a toast.

My eyes glued to Blake's and I tried to convey a world of

sorrow and love just by looking at her. I had hurt her—but, to my surprise, that didn't mean her feelings for me had disappeared. Err —so I assumed from her speech.

But maybe I'd gotten that wrong too.

Blake didn't sit again, she turned, shimming past the few guests at her table, making her way out.

Ignoring any reprimand Aunt Melanie may have wanted to send my way, I jumped up and moved across the stone floor, the quickest route to Blake.

She made it halfway around the villa before I caught up to her.

"Blake," I called. "Please wait."

"I didn't mean to ruin your cousin's party," she said, one hand flying to her face and covering her eyes.

"You didn't."

She swallowed and her chest lurched with a hitch.

Jittery from the adrenalin pumping through my body, I stepped closer, hoping she wouldn't back away. I peered down at her and wrung my hands, not allowing myself to touch her. But oh, how I wanted to touch her. "I didn't mean to hurt you. I know that sounds stupid with all the mistakes I made. But I didn't, Blake."

She dropped her hand, pressed her full lips together, and blinked up at me.

"I also didn't mean to fall in love with you. That wasn't part of my plan. But I failed that too."

"So," she huffed out a breath, her voice quiet, "you love me?"

I nodded, more afraid of her response than I'd ever been of anything in my entire life.

"But you lied to me."

"I lied to you about the festival cake, and yes, about my initial motivation to ask you out, but that's all." I crammed my eyes shut with the admission, then blinked them open. "I know that's more than enough lying. But please, Blake, believe me when I tell you the rest was real."

She nodded, but I could see she wasn't convinced. "Real or not, love hurts, Royce. It hurts so much." She wrapped her arms around her waist, hugging herself.

"Jack's right, though." I dipped my head, peering better into her eyes. "It only hurt so much—both of us by the way, I have been miserable without you—because we cared so much."

She stayed silent, listening and watching me. Her eyes studied my face, as if to reveal what I didn't say.

So—I said it. "I love you, Blake." Why did my voice have to crack that way? "Can you forgive me?" I asked—feeling like that glutton all over again, but if there was a chance, any chance at all, I had to try for it.

She lifted her bare shoulder in answer.

I let out a shaky breath, hating how desperate I felt. "Do you love me?"

She blinked and a tear slid down her smooth, blushing cheek. "I do." She stepped once toward me, lifted on the toes of her red heels, and pressed her lips to my cheek. "But I don't know if that's enough."

CHAPTER FORTY

Blake

"A month in Scotland." I looked across the table at Dad, warming my hands on my mug of herbal tea. "Did you almost stay?" I grinned at him, at his tousled salt and pepper hair, at the way his blue eyes glistened anew. "I bet you didn't want to come home."

"Of course I did," he said. "I wanted to come home, gather my girls, and go back!" He laughed and I joined him.

"I can't wait to see all your pictures."

He nodded but didn't pull out his phone. "That can wait. Family dinner on Sunday?" he said, reminding me of what I'd already agreed to.

"I'll be there."

One more affirmative nod. "Good. I'll show them to you and Jewels at the same time." His gaze flicked from the table to me. "How about you, my Blakeberry? It's been a long month for you."

I blew out an impatient breath. "Jewels has already been here, hasn't she?" That little sister of mine—she'd told Dad everything. I could see it in his face. At least I wouldn't have to explain.

"She has." He waited, his head dipped, his eyes on me.

I shrugged. "I don't know what more there is to tell."

His hand reached across for mine. "I just want my girls happy," he said. "Do—do you remember when you were sixteen and Juliana was fifteen? When that boy... Randy Don asked you to homecoming?"

I pursed my lips with the memory. Of course, I remembered. "Yes. I'd been asked, but I didn't want to go. You told Jewels she could only go if I did." I rolled my eyes. "Thanks for that, by the way."

"Why do you think I did that?" He set his face in his palm, his elbow on the table. "I'm not saying it was right... or wrong. I'm just asking, do you know why I did that?"

I threw up one hand, thinking. "Because you didn't want Juliana dating at fifteen?"

He tilted his head. "More than that. Because I was afraid," he pulled in a breath through his nostrils. "I was so afraid of someone hurting my little girls." His hand squeezed mine.

"You can't stop that from happening, Dad."

"I know that. *Now.*" He tapped his balled fist to his chin. "Do you also know why I never dated?"

I hadn't really thought about it. He was my dad—dads weren't supposed to date. But then, he was young when she left. He wasn't an old man now, really. Why didn't he? "I suppose because that chapter of your life closed when—when she left."

"Actually, that chapter didn't close. I closed it. I shut that door," his bottom lip trembled, "again out of fear."

I stood, moving my chair so that it sat flush next to his. I folded his hands inside mine. "That's understandable. You'd been hurt, terribly. No one can blame you for that."

Tilting his head, his eyes older, but still shining, beamed down at me. "I blame myself for that."

"Dad—"

"No, Blakeberry, I do. I was so afraid of loving again that I haven't lived like I should have. And now, I fear I've passed that trait down to you."

"I live," I protested, still clinging to him.

"You work. And occasionally your sister talks you into a party or a game. Neal treated you poorly. Royce made mistakes. But don't let other people's sins or weaknesses keep you from living. Really living." He brought one hand to my cheek. "Don't let the poor example of your father keep you from forgiving others and giving love a chance. Don't let all that stop you from having what you deserve."

∽

*D*istracted by the cell phone sitting on my work counter, I took my hair out of its neat ponytail, only to smooth my hair back and replace the rubber band. I paced in front of the phone, my eyes on its black screen.

I had unblocked Royce's number twelve hours ago, but he still hadn't called. The cherry blossom molds sat, ignored on the opposite side of the counter. I huffed out a breath and marched to my tools. Time to work.

And then, my phone lit with life.

Tripping over my feet, I hurried back to my cell. I lifted it up and peered down at the screen. A text from Juliana. Nibbling on my thumbnail, I read her message three times. I still wasn't sure what she said. Her words appeared jumbled and nonsensical to me. The message wasn't from *him*, so my brain didn't bother understanding.

Ignoring my sisters message, I bit my inner cheek and blew out a breath, making this more difficult than it needed to be.

I wasn't brave enough to call Royce. So, I sent a text.

You ate our donation?

Stupid, but I couldn't think of anything else to write. I waited twenty long seconds for his return. And then, it came.

Whoops. I did share.

We both knew I'd taken it to him much too early. The festival never could have used it. Three blinking dots told me he wrote again.

I'm sorry.

I gnawed on my lip, nerves sprinting inside my body. Then I typed out another text.

I guess that means you owe me.

This time his response came quick.

I guess I do.

My fingers moved fast—too fast, but autocorrect helped me send a coherent message.

I'll be working late at the shop all week. If you can, come help.

His answer came in a blink.

I'll be there.

Not even an hour later, tall, dark, and handsome walked into my shop. He stepped in, not the cocky man who'd given me a hard time at a party two months previous, but timid and nervous.

"Hey," I said, brushing the corn flour from my hands. I walked around the counter, meeting him in the open area.

"Hey," he gave me a small grin. "So, more cherry blossoms?" His furrowed brow told me Fran hadn't mentioned the job she'd offered me.

"Yeah. Fran needed a dessert vendor after all."

He nodded, but his grin broadened. I could see it made him happy that I'd be making something for the festival in the end. "So, what are you making?"

"She asked for cupcakes. I'm kind of making mini versions of my cake."

"Aww, so a cupcake too pretty to eat? Got it."

"*You* ate my cake." I smiled at him, my mind flashing back to a dozen different conversations we had about work and family, and life. And just how easy they all came—not at first, but eventually.

"I did. And I enjoyed it immensely."

I smirked out a laugh. Dad was right. I wanted to live. And dang it, I wanted to love. But more than that, I wanted to love Royce.

"Put me to work, boss. I am a pro at cherry blossom molds."

I nodded and we walked back behind the counter. I handed him the mold, the corn flour, and the modeling sugar. I'd get started on painting.

"How's work?" I asked him, grasping for normal conversation.

"Um," he paused his movement, the mold half-filled, "it's good."

I drew my brows together, studying him. "What does that mean?" I said with a light laugh.

He gave a quick shrug. "I'm mostly wrapping up with a few clients."

I set my paint brush down. Facing him, I leaned my side against the counter, so aware of his closeness, of the way his chest rose and fell with breath, of his eyes that lingered on my lips before finding my gaze. "Wrapping things up?" *The promotion.* So, strange —I didn't really know how to feel about it all. But I did know I wanted to try, and I wanted good things for Royce. "What happened with the promotion?"

He swallowed but didn't answer.

"Did Melanie offer it to you? You're wrapping up for your new job? Royce, that's... great."

Clearing his throat, he lay the mold on the counter and brushed a hand through his hair—getting corn flour on his cheek and glasses in the process. "Yeah, she offered it."

I reached out, set a hand on his shoulder, and said, "That's wonderful news. Congrats." My words came out slow and quiet— but sincere too. I hoped he could hear that. I was trying!

His feet shuffled and he inched a centimeter closer to me. "Yeah, she did offer. But I declined."

My fingers fell from his arm. "Roy!"

"I... quit, actually."

Slapping a hand over my mouth, I faced forward, away from him. "You quit?"

"I did." He still watched me, inching closer. "And crazy enough, it was the easiest decision of my life."

I twisted my neck, peering up at him, questioning his impos- sible words. He'd worked so hard. His job meant so much to him. He could have been Melanie's second!

"I couldn't take that job, Blake. Not when that job was the reason I hurt you so much. I don't want to be connected with anything that causes you pain ever again."

I licked my suddenly dried lips and blew out the breath I didn't realize I'd been holding. "Because you love me?" I whispered.

"I do." He blinked and swallowed, his gaze finding mine.

Tears welled in my eyes and spilled over onto my cheeks. I nodded. "Good. I love you, too."

He shifted, moving his body, his broad shoulders and strong chest directly in front of me. Ignoring the never-ending well of tears that spilled from my eyes, I cupped his cheek with my right palm and lifted my chin, peering up at him. Royce drew his face closer and mint and cucumber filled my senses. I thought of the time he told me I smelled of sugar and a light chuckle fell from my trembling lips.

"Blake?" he whispered, questioning my laugh.

"Oh, kiss me already, will you?"

Royce's lips parted into a grin, before crushing themselves to mine. He kissed me with urgency, and I understood. Time and trust had been lost. We were making up for both now and it felt urgent.

I needed his touch, his kiss, like I needed air. I wanted to *live*, not just be. And that meant I'd have to endure the pleasure of a thousand more kisses before I'd be satisfied.

EPILOGUE

Juliana

"*D*o you have any idea how much time she spent on that cake and now she's shoving it down his throat?" I crossed my legs, watching my sister feed her new husband.

Jack offered me a patient smile. "She's having fun. She's married—"

"Yeah, as of forty minutes ago." I sighed, chin in hand, looking at the trumpet wedding gown I designed for my sister.

Jack's fingers tangled with my own.

"And who is my dad talking to?" I peered past Blake and Royce, next to their six-tiered cake that Blake may or may not have spent six months planning, to where Dad stood with a brunette smiling at everything he said.

"That's my Aunt Nora."

"Nora?"

"Yeah remember, my mom's other sister."

My brows cinched. "The widow who lives in Georgia?"

The woman's short hair curled around her ears and she leaned into my father as if to hear him better.

I shut my eyes, unsure if I could watch the flirting happening across the room. I breathed out a sigh. It's so good—but it's so much.

Interpreting my moan wrong, Jack squeezed my fingers. "You can do this."

"I can," I said. "We *all* can. Blake can be a *wife*. Dad could be someone's *boyfriend*," my eyes went wide with the thought. "You can be floor manager," I waggled my brows at him, thinking of his new adventure. "And I—"

"*You* can do anything. You know that."

"I can," I said, my insides warm.

"You can," he repeated, "so, why not be mine—forever?"

"Jack," I began, but before I could muster any kind of answer, he pulled out a ring, a bright white pearl surrounded by diamonds.

"It's kind of been burning a hole in my pocket. But Blake's married. The cake business is booming. She's happy. According to your dad, that means it's your turn. Right?"

I blinked down at the ring pinched between his thumb and finger. "It's *our* turn because it's our time." I held back my tears and pressed a soft kiss to Jack's waiting lips. "Yes Jack, I've always known I can be anything. And I want to be yours. Forever."

HE END

Keep Reading for a sneak peak at romantic mystery: Love, In Theory.

LOVE, IN THEORY
CHAPTER ONE

*O*ne more summer semester—that's it. I can do this. I can kill myself working for one last semester. Besides, it's clinicals, it should be fun.

And then, I'll be a nurse.

I can get a job anywhere, and by anywhere, I mean far far from here.

My feet pinch with pins and needles, and though my dad's house is only a mile away, I wish for the thousandth time that I could afford a car.

But I can't.

And Dad won't buy me one. I offended him by declaring myself independent at eighteen, three long years ago. Not that I would be able to afford gas for a car, anyway.

Crack! I jump, stopping my march home. "Firecrackers? In May?" My voice echoes into the dark, midnight, moonless night. "It's nothing Lydia," I tell myself. "You spent too many years in the slums of Denver. Cheyenne is safe."

An owl hoots, disliking the noise as much as I had. I jerk again with his call, spurring my feet back into gear. Still, who would shoot off fireworks in May?

My heart thunders in my ears, the question ringing again and again through my head. I can't make any sense of it. Paranoid, I repeat one of the lectures Dad gave to me two years ago:

"Cheyenne is safe, Lydia. It's a small town. Wouldn't you like to try out a small town? Small and safe."

It wasn't the "safe" talk that enticed me, but when he baited me with free room and board and a college that had already accepted my application. I thought it a wise decision—even if I had to live with his new wife—*Tina.*

Sure, the lecture may not have enticed me here, but it is what I'm recalling at this very midnight moment. I spent four late hours in the school library. When the library closed and kicked me out, I studied in the lobby of Al's dorm. The dorm locks everything up at midnight—my cue to leave. So, I left, on this moonless night, for my mile walk home.

My feet *tap-tap* on the sidewalk, the only sound besides the owl and that one firework. I count my steps in my head, ignoring the quiet and bleakness around me. Through the dim street lamps, I can just make out the obscure windows of the businesses on both sides of the road. There are closed signs in every window and they all seem to hold dark shadows and creepy secrets. I shiver, my doom and gloom head giving the innocent surroundings a frightening feel—all over one firework.

I straighten my shoulders; I can walk home at midnight. I'm a big girl. I spent the entire twenty-one years of my life being *the* adult. So, I can be an adult now. I can walk home in this *safe, small* town. Right?

Pop!

This time the noise rings louder and sharper—and sounds less like a firework. I pull my light gray jacket tighter around me and peer to the left, just past one of the old buildings on Oak Street. It had once been a five and dime store. I've seen the old sign a hundred times on my walks home. The thrift shop it transformed into never took the original sign down. Another faceless, made-up shadow looms through the five and dime window. I stop, my feet glued to the ground, staring into the dark pane, my brain echoing the *pop* I heard.

A movement through the dirty pane causes my body to freeze and my breath to quiver—that wasn't my imagination. I gasp, pulling in air though my lungs want to quit on me. I adjust the backpack, loaded with books, on my shoulders. My eyes fix on the store window. There's nothing—until suddenly a figure falls against the pane with a thud. The person's back presses into the window. My eyes stay open and glued to the spot where he stands, where his body is flush to the glass. I can't stop looking. Another pop has me blinking, but still I keep the figure in focus. Why won't my feet move? Why can't I stop gawking this way?

The figure begins to move, but it's unnatural. He—I'm sure it's a he now—slides down the five and dime window pane, leaving a streak, red as a rose, as a ruby—as blood—across the already filthy pane. A faceless, surely fictional, figure appears where the man once stood. The form lifts a hand and it pangs against the window, making me jerk and move for the first time in probably two solid minutes. The face attached to the body is a blur, but my eyes find the gun, it's clear and crisp through my tunneled sight.

Fear catches in my throat—though I want to scream—and my vision swims. My head stings with a fuzziness that comes before a migraine.

A gun. An actual gun. Not imaginary, I think as my brain tries to process the last three minutes.

Two faceless men.

Pops.

And blood.

So. Much. Blood.

I don't fear blood. My instinct has always been to rush toward it—but the *gun.* That, petrifies me in place. I stare at the revolver, still pressing against the window, right next to the streak of crimson.

Noise breaks through the quiet night once more, this time with words, though my brain doesn't compute what's been said through the barrier of the building. I blink, looking up from the gun to the faceless man—who all at once has features. Blurry, shadowy features. A dark line stamps along his jaw and I study it—trying to understand it—until I lift my gaze to bright eyes, staring directly at me.

Click here to keep reading!

THANK YOU & FREEBIE!

Thank you for reading *Romancing Blake.* I hope that you enjoyed it.

If you'd like more information on my novels or other clean reads, you can sign up for my weekly newsletter. I share deals and fun reads once a week. For signing up you'll receive a free copy of my novel, *Then Came You.*

Love,

Jen

Receive your free gift here!

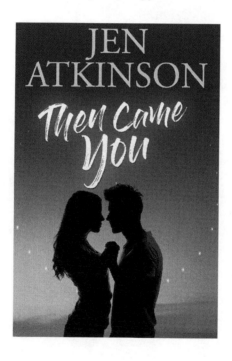

ACKNOWLEDGMENTS

Thank you to Samantha, LeeAnn, & Kristol for reading this book in it's early and semi scary stages! I appreciate your help, love, and critiques more than you know! I am so blessed to call each of you friend.

As always, huge thanks to my family for patience, love, and support while I write myself a love story.

Thank you to my readers and fellow sweet romcom authors! I love you! Special thanks to my Bookstagram friends who have supported and promoted Romancing Blake. I appreciate yo so much!

Lastly, I'm grateful God has called me to write. It's a little romance story. But my hope and prayer is that at the end of this book—and all of my books—my readers feel uplifted and joyful. I feel really blessed to know that God loves me and all of you—and that He wants us all to find some joy.

ABOUT THE AUTHOR

Jen Atkinson is a born and raised Wyoming girl who believes there is no better place on earth. Jen fills her days raising kids, dating her husband, working with elementary students, and of course, writing swoon-worthy romance. She loves reading a good, clean, love story as well as a young adult dystopian.

Jen lives next to one of Wyoming's many mountains where the wind regularly whips through her hair and bites at her cheeks. Her greatest loves are her four children, Timothy, Landon, Seth, and Sydney, as well as her husband Jeff. She is the author of several clean romance novels, including *The Amelia Chronicles* and *The Untouched Trilogy.*

Photo by Halle Garrett
Photography